Praise for Eden Maguire

"The hip, young living dead in Eden Maguire's *Twilight*-ish new book series Beautiful Dead are totally cool."

—*Seventeen*

"Emotional confrontations, sweet interludes between the lovers, and adrenaline-surging moments of physical threat...Fans of the *Twilight* franchise and shows like *Supernatural* should be an eager audience."

—*Publishers Weekly*

"The combination of mystery, the supernatural, and romance is enough to keep the reader interested."

—*VOYA*

PHOENIX

BEAUTIFUL DEAD

Eden Maguire

sourcebooks
fire

Published by Sourcebooks Fire, an imprint of Sourcebooks, Inc.
P.O. Box 4410, Naperville, Illinois 60567-4410
(630) 961-3900
Fax: (630) 961-2168
teenfire.sourcebooks.com

First published in Great Britain in 2010 by Hodder Children's Books.

Library of Congress Cataloging-in-Publication data is on file with the publisher.

Printed and bound in the United States of America.
VP 10 9 8 7 6 5 4 3 2 1

For my two beautiful daughters

Maybe none of it is true.

I reach the end, and I wimp out: "I woke up, and it was all a dream."

Imagine that—I made up the Beautiful Dead, the whole thing. Jonas, Arizona, Summer, and Phoenix out at Foxton Ridge. I did it because I wanted them back in my life so bad. But there really is no such being as Hunter the overlord, no zombie stepping out of limbo back to the far side—nothing except me and my crazy, grief-fueled brain.

I play Summer Madison's song as I drive a winding road, late-spring aspens rising silver and green to either side.

"I love you so, but it was time to go. You spoke my name, I never came, 'cause it was time for me to go."

He's dead, I tell myself. Beautiful Phoenix, every day you break my heart. Your eyes stare into mine but not really. You hold my hand, and it's cold as death.

"You spoke my name, I never came, 'cause it was time for me to go."

I drive into the mountains. The roof is down. I feel the wind in my hair. Mid-May and the aspen leaves shake and shimmer in the breeze. Hot sun bakes my face, and the sandy soil, the dirt track crunches under my tires. I hit a sudden hollow, the CD jumps and sticks—"t-t-time for m-me to go..." I press the off button. Where am I heading? Who do I hope to see? Half a mile from Foxton Ridge I brake suddenly. The engine stalls.

I'm half a mile from Angel Rock and that steep dip into the hidden valley where the spring meadow surrounds the empty barn and the old ranch house. Scarlet poppies sing and zing in the fresh green grass, a wave of wind rolls through and sighs up dust in the deserted yard.

In the silence after the engine cuts out I'm unable to act. I sit trapped by invisible threads of memory and hope.

We never needed to talk, Phoenix and me. I would look into those gray-blue eyes and know—just know—what he was thinking. I remember the way he would push his dark hair clear of his forehead, once, twice, three times, without knowing he was doing it. And I would lift my hand to do it for him, then he would smile. That smile—raised higher on the right-hand side, uneven, quirky. The love light in his eyes.

Inside my silver memory cocoon I sit. Should I reach out and turn on the engine? I see myself coming to the end of the track, getting out of the car, walking into the shade of the rusting water tower, and pausing to gaze down at the barn. The barn will cast a long shadow across the yard. The door will hang open. Nailed above the door will be the moose antlers. Beside it, and in the old corral beyond, pure blue columbines will stand out among dark, straggly thornbushes.

No footsteps will disturb decades of untrodden dirt; no movement, no sound.

I know—I've done this so many times.

Once, twice, three times I walk down to the barn and peer inside. "Be here!" I breathe.

My heart batters my rib cage.

Four, five, six times I make out spiky farm tools stacked in a corner, horse halters hanging like nooses, an avalanche of decaying straw.

Seven, eight times I turn away. Maybe in the ranch house?

"Be here!" I cross the yard and step up onto the porch. The old boards creak. I press my face to the windowpane. "Be here!"

Nine, ten times the stove is there, the table and rocking chair, the plates on the rack. And undisturbed dust. I don't even try the door—I know it's bolted on the inside.

Twenty times I've gone through this ritual of hope.

Now the rocking chair will rock, now the plates will be taken down from the rack, a fire will heat the stove. Someone will come down the stairs and into the tiny kitchen—stern, serious Hunter, who built this place a hundred years ago and who died here—will throw another log on the fire. He will turn to speak to someone in the shadows. A tall figure will step out.

I know every inch of this person—the broad shoulders, the thick dark hair, high forehead, and lopsided smile. Now I will whisper his name. "Phoenix."

I can't do it, I tell myself this twenty-first time.

I sit in my car for a whole hour. Deer walk out from under the aspens. They lower their heads and graze. High in the blue sky a plane gleams silver, small as an insect.

One more disappointment and my heart will stutter to a halt.

Phoenix is dead and gone forever, along with Summer Madison, Jonas Jonson, and Arizona Taylor. The Beautiful Dead are imagined.

I switch on the engine, reverse down the track, turn, and head back to the highway.

Wednesday, I drove to school with conjoined Jordan and Lucas. These days they're the real deal, can't keep their hands off each other, limbs permanently intertwined—and I'm jealous.

I was sitting in the backseat, recalling how Phoenix and I used to be the same way.

"Darina, what happened to your car?" Jordan asked, letting go of Lucas just long enough to turn around and ask the question. "Did Brandon take it back?"

"Yeah, but only for a service." Shiny red, creamy leather girl-mobile with a fold-down top—gift of Phoenix's big brother, Brandon Rohr. "It feels like someone amputated a leg."

"When do you get it back?" Lucas wanted to know.

I'm amazed by Lucas. Six months ago, he was the shy guy in the corner. It's like Clark Kent going into the phone booth and coming out with a cape and a six-pack.

New-look, bulked-up Lucas doesn't hide—he stares you right in the eye, even through the overhead mirror.

"Friday," I muttered.

"So I'll give you a ride home," he offered as he pulled into the school parking lot.

"Thanks."

"Hey, Darina, I'm thinking about cutting my hair." Jordan got out of the car and tossed her luscious dark locks back from her face.

"Don't," I advised. "Your hair is your best feature."

"Just this much?"

"Oh yeah, that much—cool."

"Are you letting yours grow?"

"No, I have an appointment with my hairdresser Monday."

My hair isn't my best feature. If I have one, it would be my eyes—definitely according to Phoenix. I wear a lot of kohl and mascara so people notice. I think I knew from the age of seven I was never going to be the floaty hair type.

I spotted Hannah down the corridor and left the love-birds to it. "Hey," I said.

Hannah waited for me to catch up. "What happened to you?"

"When?"

"Yesterday evening. We were at the pool, remember?"

"I forgot."

Not really. I'd looked out at the sun and blue sky and knew I wasn't in bikini mood. I could've driven out to

Foxton instead but decided against that, too, in case it turned out to be another lonely, wasted journey.

("It's a great evening. How come you're not going out?" my mom, Laura, had asked. I'd offered no answer, only my sullen stare.)

"Zoey was there, poolside."

"Cool. How's she doing?" We turned into the classroom, which was almost empty.

"Good. She plans to be back in school full-time in the fall."

Talking and paying attention takes a lot of energy when all you want to do is not be there. As a matter of fact, I didn't think I would make it through the day.

"She'll repeat the year. Her physical therapist says that swimming is the best workout for her, better even than horse riding." Hannah didn't care that I'd slumped down at my desk and was faking concentration on my laptop. "It strengthens her leg muscles—the ones she still needs to work on. She's put on a little weight, which is a good thing, but she stresses about it being too much, and Jordan and I kept saying she's still a size zero, so no way."

I glanced up from my computer. For a split second I saw Phoenix across the room.

❧

"You're home early."

Laura has a knack of turning everything into an accusation.

3

"Yeah, major criminal offense." I wanted to flounce out of the kitchen and slam the door.

"How did you get here?"

"I have legs."

"You walked?"

"Yeah, Mom—W-A-L-K-E-D." I'd hung in there at school for as long as I could, looking for Phoenix around every corner, down the corridors, out the main entrance, along the street, in the coffee shop in the main shopping mall. He didn't show up after that nano-glimpse in the classroom, over in less than the blink of an eye.

Enough to fall in love with the beautiful ghost in the corner all over again.

But now Laura was in the mood for talking. T-A-L-K-ing. She had that serious I-know-how-you-feel expression.

She didn't, of course. How could she? She hadn't lost a boyfriend in a gang fight and never found out who had pushed the knife between his shoulder blades. She didn't commune with the dead.

"Darina, it's almost a year."

Don't say that! Don't remind me!

"The anniversary—it's gonna be tough."

My mom thinks I'm totally screwed up. She wants me to be over Phoenix, has even talked about us moving out of Ellerton, away from the memories. My stepdad, Jim, says we can relocate anywhere, he can base his job in any city in the entire country. They called in a realtor to put the house on the market. Luckily no one's buying.

"You could see Kim Reiss again," Laura suggested.

"Been there, got the T-shirt." My last therapy session had been in early spring—the start of April. I was always surprised that I liked Kim, but still not enough right now to go back.

"It'll help you over the twelve-month hurdle."

I was seconds away from door-slam time. "No, Mom, it won't." Seeing a therapist wasn't on my anniversary list, where there was actually only one item—to find the courage to get back out to Foxton before it was too late.

"Please, honey—at least think about it."

If I step into that barn one more time and Phoenix isn't there…If I try the door to the ranch house and it's locked…my heart stops dead.

"Darina?"

I shook my head and took the stairs two at a time. I threw myself down on my bed and pulled the pillow over my head.

Love doesn't end just because I'm not around.

It's Phoenix's voice I hear this time, even though I can't see his face.

Every time you think of me—that's love. Every sunset. Every diamond drop of water in Deer Creek. That's love.

The car came back on Friday, detailed outside and in. Brandon showed up a few minutes later.

"It's got new front tires," he told me, plus he'd made sure the service guys delivered it personally right to my door.

I was alone in the house. "You want a coffee?"

"Beer."

I raided Jim's stash in the garage—the locally brewed stuff he keeps for special occasions. Brandon stayed outside on the porch. Here's the thing with Brandon—like him or loathe him, you can't ignore him. It's a physical aura, not muscle and bone exactly, more a strong, dark presence. His eyes suspect everyone and everything.

"How's your mom?" I asked, for something to say. Crap—why hadn't I just taken the car keys from him and said thanks and good-bye?

He shook his head, dismissing the question like a wet dog shaking water from its back.

"And Zak?" Dig a hole, then dig it deeper. Actually, I knew Zak had recently been expelled from school.

Beer can in hand, Brandon took a deep breath. "My family is doing great, Darina. My mom, my brother— thank you for asking." He does sarcastic better than most.

"OK, sorry."

Back to the Brandon aura—he gives off the impression that he's invincible, ten times stronger than the next guy, a hundred times tougher, with no chinks in his armor. Then there's the rumored links with the Ellerton drug gangs, the Harley parked by the curb, and the leather jacket.

"So your car's good for another twelve months," he told me as he stood the empty can on the rail. "Call me if you need anything."

You have to understand—he didn't say it because he cared, but because he'd sworn to Phoenix as Phoenix lay dying that he'd take care of me. It's a sense of family honor so strong that I'm guessing Brandon would rather die himself than break that promise.

"I don't—need anything."

He stared at me. His eyes were nothing like his brother's so my heart didn't thump and jump like it did when Brandon smiled, because his mouth *was* the same.

"Only for Phoenix to still be here," I confessed. The quick smile hanging off the end of Brandon's intense stare dragged the comment out of me. *Weak moment, black mark, Darina.*

Brandon shut off the smile, raised his eyebrows, and shrugged. He rode off on his Harley.

I turned and went into the kitchen. Phoenix sat at the table, watching me. I gasped, closed my eyes, opened them, and he was gone.

Every time I got behind the wheel of my car, ninety-nine percent of me longed to turn it toward Foxton.

"You want to play tennis?" Hannah asked the next day. She'd driven along my street, tennis bag at the ready.

"Are you crazy?" I hadn't picked up a racket in three years—didn't she know that?

"Hitting practice would be good—let out some aggression," said blonde Hannah, sleek and long-legged in her white tennis skirt.

"I have no aggression," I argued and turned my back.

"Who drank my special beer?" Jim was standing on the porch holding up the empty can that I'd left there on purpose from the day before to annoy him.

The weekend passed, and I didn't even make it into school on Monday. I sat in my room ignoring text messages from Hannah and Jordan, checking my calendar as if I didn't already know that it was eleven days.

A message came through on my phone from Laura: MADE APPOINTMENT WITH KIM. WEDNESDAY 4:30 P.M. I called her back. "What part of *no* don't you understand?"

Three hundred and fifty-four days since Phoenix was killed. Eleven more and the year was up.

HAIRDRESSER TODAY, 3:00 P.M. Laura texted a reminder.

That's almost two decades of running my life for me.

I showed up at the hairdresser's because I was going nuts staying in my room.

"Hey, Darina." A lipstick smile and a waft of scented shampoo/conditioner/hair spray greeted me as I opened the door. Warm air, lilac and silver walls, the drone of driers. "Go through. Kristal is ready for you."

You really have to trust your hairdresser with her pointy scissors. Kristal hadn't cut my hair before today, so I had to tell her how I like it to look—chin-length, straight, choppy. I hoped she was giving it her full attention.

She shampooed and toweled, sat me down in front of her mirror, knew from the look on my face not to ask me questions about my day. With my wet hair combed back and sticking to my scalp I looked all of eight years old.

Half an hour later, moussed and sprayed, I was saying thanks and meaning it. I now looked old enough to drive— Kristal could cut my hair whenever she liked.

And soon I was driving out of town through Centennial, following the route Jonas had ridden with Zoey on the day he crashed, thinking only about the Beautiful Dead. Summer was singing on my sound system, her angel voice living on. And Arizona was in my head, not directly telling me that I was letting Phoenix down, but the truth was coming through because she couldn't hide the disappointment she felt. Arizona always told it like it was.

"I can't do it!" I whispered. My hands on the steering wheel were white at the knuckles, the skin stretched tight. "I don't have the courage!"

You were there for me, Arizona-inside-my-head said. *You saved my immortal soul. And let's face it, Darina, you didn't even like me.*

"That's why."

So now the opposite. You can't save Phoenix because you love him too much and always will? You're telling me that's why you haven't the courage to help him?

"Yes. Because what if I fail?"

Don't think that way. Believe in yourself.

"Eleven days." I don't know if I even whispered this out loud. *Eleven days then his time is done.*

"I go to Foxton, and he's not there. I look everywhere— he's never there."

Look again, said Arizona-in-my-head.

"I can't—I'm too afraid!"

I turned the car down a side street, away from the inter- state and the Foxton junction. Across the street, standing in front of a picket fence, under a white blossom tree, I see Phoenix. He's watching me, waiting for me to come.

❧

"You don't go out. You don't see anyone anymore." Laura was on my case again.

Silence from me. I'd fixed my hair so it didn't look like I'd just walked out of the salon. Jim wasn't home from work yet, so Laura had free range. She sat beside me at the kitchen table. "I see you have some down time. Why not call Jordan, find out if she wants to watch a movie?"

"Jordan is welded to Lucas twenty-four/seven." It hadn't taken her long to move on from Logan to her new man, but like I said, Lucas has recently become a hunk, so I didn't really blame her.

"Call Hannah."

No reply. Maybe Laura would hit her head against my wall of silence and admit defeat.

But no—she came at me from the side. "You'll definitely go and see Kim on Wednesday?"

I shrugged. There wasn't a therapist alive who could drag me out of the pit I was in.

"Promise me?"

"OK." I threw a little scrap of cooperation into the mix to make her back off. I even tried to smile as I got up and went upstairs in time to avoid Jim as his car drew up outside.

❧

The low sun shone directly into my room, reminding me it was early summer. Long, light evenings loomed—and more memories. The season had been ours, Phoenix's and mine, the heat prickling our skin as we sat by Deer Creek, the delicious coldness of the water when we dipped our feet. We would take off our clothes and swim. I closed the curtains, lay on the bed.

Downstairs, Laura told Jim that I'd agreed to see the shrink.

WHERE U HIDIN? A text came through from Zoey.

HOW U DOIN? I texted back.

DON'T CHANGE SUBJECT. DO U NEED TO TALK?

THNX BUT NO THNX. SEE U IN SCHOOL 2MORO.

The sun had sunk behind the mountains, and my room was cooling. I lay without moving until it got dark.

Being in love with a dead person is similar to what happens when a fox is caught in a trap. The fox steps into the snare in the dead of night. *Click*—the trap closes on its foot, the saw-edge blade tears the flesh to the bone. The fox howls in pain, sees the blood, whimpers, and endures.

Daylight drives it crazy. It begins to bite and gnaw at the trapped leg. Sometimes it bites off its own foot just to be free.

The Beautiful Dead don't exist. I lay on the bed and made my last desperate bid for freedom. *I'll see Kim Reiss, tell her everything—how crazy I've been for almost a year, how I invented a whole story to keep me close to Phoenix, a fantasy world, and I've been wearing it like a bandage over the still-gaping wound.*

Darkness surrounded me. Outside the window, a breeze started to blow.

I'll do it Wednesday—unpick this crazy secret and let Kim heal me.

There would be a diagnosis and a cure. She would talk about post-traumatic stress and talking therapy, cognitive behavior methods, the value of good diet and exercise. I'd googled the topic so I already had the answers.

In the future, when I fell into negative thought patterns, I would catch myself doing it, put on my sweats, and go for a healthy run.

It's gonna take more than pulling on a pair of jogging pants, I would tell Kim. She would smile that friendly smile and say we had to start somewhere.

"Night, honey," Laura called through my door as she and Jim went to bed.

I switched off my light and let the darkness lap over me. The wind strengthened. There was going to be a storm.

I'll tell Kim about my visions, and I'll be free, I told myself. *Run, run, run.*

It was past midnight. My curtains billowed in the wind. I got up from my bed to close the window.

"We need to talk," Hunter said.

✦❖✦

The first time I saw Hunter he was a man of stone. You would have thought his features had been chiseled—there was no flicker of expression on his stern face.

The second time I saw him I thought he was made of iron. Then steel. Think of any material that is unbending and cold. He has gray eyes that see everything, gray hair swept back from his face, a fading angel-wing tattoo on his forehead. "We need to talk," he told me now.

And the wind blew into the room and filled it like a million beating wings.

I stood by the window struggling for breath, only half seeing Hunter in the shadows, behind the Beautiful Dead shield of wings.

"Sit down, Darina," he said quietly. "Don't say anything until you get your thoughts together.

Don't do this to me! I pleaded. *Don't start the whole thing up again!*

"I've been waiting, watching," he told me.

And I've come to Foxton looking for you, I really have!

"I know it," he said, without me having to speak.

I stood up, but he forced me to sit again with just a look. My legs folded under me, and I was sitting on the bed. "Were you there—at Foxton—all along?" I whispered.

"There was always someone—Dean, Iceman, me...OK, I know—so why didn't we let you know?" Hunter was at least two steps ahead. I underestimated that mind-reading power of his. "Let's say it was a trial period."

"What is this—an *exam?* After all that I've done, I still have to pass a test!"

"Dean and Iceman—they were under orders from me not to show themselves, only to observe."

There, in my dark room, I recalled my recent visits to the ranch house—the stillness except for the barn door banging, destroying my hopes. "Do you have any idea how cruel that is?"

"To observe you and test your courage." If Hunter heard my question he deflected it—*ping*, like an arrow off a shield. "I had to know if you have the strength to help Phoenix."

I raised my head and held his gaze. *OK, is that why you're here—to tell me I failed the test? To zap my memory clear of the Beautiful Dead? So that's a heap of Laura's money saved on seeing a therapist.*

"I'm not here to condemn you, Darina. I'm here to talk." Hunter stepped toward me, his eyes searching my face. "And you must know that the Beautiful Dead don't show themselves to you unless it's absolutely necessary and only after we've exhausted every other avenue."

It was true—getting in touch with me was never their first choice, and I knew why. Making contact with people from the far side was always a big risk to their existence.

15

"What else did you try?" I whispered.

"Dean—you remember Dean—he went to Henry Jardine's office and learned all he could from the police records of the investigation."

Dean was an ex-cop. I hardly knew him—only that he was Beautiful Dead and had been given the chance to return to the far side because of the way he died in a hit-and-run car crash. That and the fact that he was due to become an overlord once Hunter's job was done.

"Did he find anything new?" I asked.

"Not much. They never even identified the knife that killed Phoenix, let alone his attacker. They interviewed the gas station cashier, plus a dozen other witnesses. The case is still open, but there are no fresh leads."

"No weapon," I murmured. And I pictured the chaos of the fight on the forecourt—Brandon and his gang versus a group of out-of-town bikers, Phoenix stepping in possibly to help his brother, getting stabbed in the back.

"Most of the witnesses refused to cooperate with the cops. They closed ranks."

"What about Brandon?" I asked.

Hunter watched my every move. He noticed the struggle I was going through to keep my voice level, to stop my hands from shaking. "Brandon was the exception. In his interview with Deputy Sheriff Jardine he provided names, gave a description of the build up to the fight, the duration, the types of weapons used."

"But nothing that led the cops to the identity of the killer?"

"The file is still open, case unsolved," he reminded me. I let a long silence develop.

"I know, Darina—this is hard." Hunter joined me at the window. He drew back the curtains and stared out.

I closed my eyes. "Sure, you read minds. You know I'm terrified. But how deep do you see? Can you work out exactly why I've stayed away?"

"You're scared you'll fail, that you won't solve Phoenix's killing."

"Yeah, that's one reason." I wasn't sure where I was going with this, whether Hunter was even interested, but I stumbled on. "You know when love and loss overwhelm you? You ache from it, it fogs your brain, you're caught in its trap."

Hunter stood very close, very pale and cold. "I do understand. I lost my wife to Peter Mentone," he reminded me.

A hundred years ago, in the room with the stove and the rocking chair, with the blood stain on the floor. I knew the whole story.

Hunter did something surprising—he reached into his shirt pocket and pulled out a faded picture. He showed it to me but didn't let go.

"This is Marie?" I couldn't help it—I was trembling, wanting to cry as I looked at the brown and white, curling-at-the-edges photo. I saw straightaway what Arizona and Summer meant when they said I reminded Hunter of his dead wife. Her hair was dark, her mouth was wide, you noticed her eyes.

"Mentone was our neighbor, out beyond Angel Rock. He lived alone, ran a few cattle, drank in the bar at Foxton. He was a guy you didn't want to spend time with."

"You don't need to explain." It seemed wrong—Hunter the overlord opening up to me, sharing his tragedy.

In the half-light of the moon appearing from behind a bank of clouds I stared at the faded angel-wing tattoo on his forehead.

He gazed at the sky as he slid the picture back in his pocket. "Marie thought different—she was too soft-hearted. She felt sorry for the guy, said she didn't like to think of him all alone in the shack he called home. Once in a while she invited him to supper. He misinterpreted that, I guess."

"You don't need to…" I breathed.

"We talked about it. I said I didn't like the way Mentone looked at her. Marie said not to worry, it was nothing she couldn't handle. I let it go."

Startled, I looked straight at Hunter. "You're not blaming yourself?" The way I'd heard it, Mentone had broken in on Marie while Hunter was out. He'd gone right in there and raped her. Hunter had come back unexpectedly, torn Mentone off his wife. Mentone had pulled a gun and shot Hunter through the head. "They had a trial. They hanged him."

"I shouldn't have let it go. I should've been there for her."

Now, unlike the Beautiful Dead, I'm no mind reader, but when Hunter came to a sudden halt, I knew there was more he wanted to say.

"It was *not* your fault," I insisted. Then my mind did a backflip, and I focused on the phrase he'd used—*I lost my wife to Peter Mentone.*

The moon disappeared behind the clouds: Hunter and I were in the dark.

"Overwhelmed by loss." He sighed.

They tried Mentone, and they hanged him. Where was the mystery in that? Why had Hunter been chosen to come back as leader of the Beautiful Dead?

"The feelings don't stop when you die," he explained. "You carry them with you. Limbo is a place of tortured souls, all looking for answers—for decades, for centuries, until the end of time. The lucky ones get to come back to the far side to solve their mysteries."

"You said you lost Marie to Mentone? What did you mean?"

"She had a child—a girl."

"I know—Marie named her Hester. I read about her in the newspaper archive."

Hunter was set on telling me every detail, and he continued along that road. "There were rumors. They said she was Mentone's daughter, not mine. They wanted Marie to give her up for adoption." He spoke the painful words in a noncomprehending, almost detached voice.

"But she didn't. She kept Hester and brought her up, sent her to school, got her an education." I read that, too.

"They blamed her for doing that, said she wasn't fit to be around decent folks."

We'd reached the heart of Hunter's mystery, and I asked the core question. "And all this time you haven't known—was Hester yours or Mentone's?"

It was Hunter's turn to let the long silence develop between us. "Worse," he admitted at last. "Was that really rape I walked in on, or did my wife consent?"

If I knew one thing, it was that Phoenix loved me. Without question, he loved me with all his heart. I hung on to that knowledge through the dark days after he died, through the funeral, and all the crazy weeks when I drove into the mountains looking for comfort and found it in that dark barn at Foxton whenever the Beautiful Dead appeared.

"And now, Darina, you have to make a decision." Hunter had been patient with me, sharing his own doubts, his mysteries, but he was here for another reason. "Which way does your love for Phoenix take you? Will you work with us again, or do you prefer to walk away?"

I stood at the dark window. I took in the details of my room—the silver necklace hanging from my mirror, the tubes and pots of cosmetics on my table, the impression of my head on the pillow. My gaze swung past Hunter, no longer a man of stone or steel, toward the sky.

Wings beat against the windowpane. Eleven days minus one—ten, because we were past midnight.

"Well?" Hunter asked.

"I lost him once," I whispered. "And now I have to lose him again."

"Or you could forget."

"You would do that?"

He nodded. "You've seen how it works. I can take your memories of Phoenix and the Beautiful Dead, and I can erase them completely. You can get on with your life."

"There'd be nothing left? No Foxton, no barn, no rituals? I would drive out there and find no trace?"

"Nothing," he promised, fixing me with that deep-down stare. "None of this would ever have happened."

"Only memories of Phoenix and me together before he died, the good times?"

"Yes."

EDEN MAGUIRE

I would be like Zoey, learning to live without Jonas, putting one foot in front of another. Like Summer's parents, Heather and Jon Madison, listening to her music, remembering.

"Would I be happy?" I wanted to know.

Hunter's gaze flickered. "I can't say."

"Sorry—stupid question."

"*Good* question," he insisted. "Phoenix would want you to be."

Phoenix. To me, even his name sounds like a sigh, like wind in the aspens. I held my breath.

"Walk away and be happy?" Hunter prompted.

"I could never do that," I said.

2

I told Hunter I would drive out to Foxton early the next morning. He promised me Phoenix would be there.

As he was about to leave, an idea popped into my head and, without stopping to think it through, I offered it to him. "I could follow up with what happened to Marie and Hester."

He recoiled and acted like I'd shot him in the head all over again. "Why would I want you to do that?"

"To find out if they were—well, happy. Wouldn't you like to know?"

"Happy?" he echoed. That word again. Without giving me an answer, he turned his focus inward, created the shimmering halo from head to foot, and dissolved into nothing.

At least he didn't say no, I thought.

And I kept myself busy during the long hours before dawn by planning how I would do the research—go back to the website where I'd read the history of Ellerton, type in the early twentieth-century date when Hunter was killed and Peter Mentone was tried and hanged—get all the facts, refresh my memory. After that I would type in Marie Lee's name and see what came up. Marie was a teacher before she married small-time rancher Hunter Lee, I remembered. Maybe she went back to teaching after he died. Maybe she kept Hester and moved a million miles away from this narrow-minded small town to make a new life in the city. Or maybe she did give her daughter up for adoption in the end.

I only toyed with the life-story-of-Marie-and-Hester idea because it kept me from obsessing over my Foxton trip.

Even so, the night crawled by and other unruly thoughts kept breaking in.

"Tell Darina I'm sorry." It was Phoenix's voice saying this, and my mental picture was of him lying in his own blood with Brandon bending over him. "Tell Darina I'm sorry."

They were the last words Phoenix spoke.

Flashback number two: "Who killed him?" This was me asking Brandon the question that never got answered.

We were in my old car, sitting outside Brandon's apartment. Brandon wasn't giving me anything back. He was blocking me. "Were you ever in a fight?" he said. "There were twelve or more guys. Kicking, punching, shoving. Someone pulled a knife. That's all I know."

More flashes, more unwelcome pictures before dawn, of me standing next to Logan Lavelle, staring down at a patch of Phoenix's blood. An empty gas station with red and green neon signs, no sound except the crime scene plastic tape flapping.

Me refusing to believe that Phoenix didn't make it to the hospital, that I would never see him again. My whole life torn apart.

The minutes crept by. Come first light, I was out of the house. I heard Laura rush to the door in her robe, too late to stop me from driving away.

How often in the last twelve months had I followed this road out to the Beautiful Dead? First for Jonas, then for Arizona, and earlier this spring for Summer—sometimes eager and hopeful, more times in despair.

The best occasions would be driving when I had news for them, fresh information, a detail that would rescue each of them from everlasting limbo. The worst were full of doubt—crazy-girl, deluded Darina driving out to Foxton in a rainstorm because she couldn't, wouldn't accept that Phoenix was gone.

I drove through Centennial onto the interstate, gained altitude, felt the granite mountain slopes rise steeply to either side of the winding road. I was in the shadow of Turkey Shoot Ridge where Jonas died, glancing down on Hartmann Lake in the distance, perfect in the early sun. I glanced at my watch and calculated that I would reach Foxton Ridge by seven A.M.

Today, ten days before Phoenix's deadline, was I hopeful girl or was I crazy, delusional Darina? Somewhere in between, with nerves stretched to a breaking point, wishing every second that the drive was over and that I was in Phoenix's arms.

I reached the lightning-stricken pine trees that line the road as you come into Foxton junction, glimpsed a couple of new Western-style luxury buildings high on a hill, and signaled left at the old grocery store onto the dirt track by the creek.

My car kicked up clouds of dust, hit a hollow, bounced, and veered toward the cliff edge, giving me a snatched view of the white-water rapids below. I steered it back on track past the fishermen's shacks—on, on toward Foxton Ridge.

Hunter had promised that Phoenix would be there, waiting for me. I'd already glimpsed him in the classroom, in my kitchen, standing by the picket fence. He'd been there an instant then faded. In the heartbeat after he'd disappeared, I'd sensed his massive disappointment in me for turning my back on him.

Sorry, so sorry, my love! I put my foot on the gas, sped recklessly toward the ridge. At the end of the track, I jumped out of the car and ran through the silky green grass.

You need me—I know you do. More than ever before.

Here was the stand of aspens and the rusty water tower, there was the valley, the poppy-strewn hill sweeping down toward the ranch house and the barn.

Please, Phoenix, don't tell me that I'm too late!

I paused for breath, stared at the truck abandoned down the side of the house with two wheels missing, the hood dented, the glass in the windshield cracked and crazed. I looked from there to the big barn, so old and weathered that it almost looked like part of the landscape. I saw weeds springing up outside the open door, the giant moose horns branching above.

Not too late, please!

I wanted wings to start beating, a barrier to keep me out, to tell me the Beautiful Dead were back.

"You promised," I told Hunter out loud.

But there was warmth and sun—no wind, no wings as I set off again down the hillside.

I'd made maybe ten strides when a voice called out.

It came from the ridge so I stopped and turned. There was a man—a deer hunter or a hiker dressed in jeans and a plaid shirt hanging open over a white T-shirt—standing by the open door of a silver SUV. He must have driven off-road and was maybe curious to find out why I abandoned my car in this deserted spot.

"We need to talk!" he yelled.

Bad timing, mister! I'd been building up to this visit for weeks and didn't want a stranger interfering with my big reunion. But what could I do? I had to walk back up the hill and throw him off the scent.

"You don't know me," he said as I drew near. "But I know you."

I broke my stride and frowned at him. "Are you following me?"

"Coincidence. I was up early, driving in your neighborhood. I knew your car."

"You knew my car?" If I was feeling uneasy before, double it now that I got a clear view of the guy. He was tall, late forties, and I felt as though I'd seen him before.

"A red convertible. Zak told me."

"Zak?" Since when did I develop this parrot habit?

"It fits," he said, looking me up and down. "You would be Phoenix's type of girl."

My eyes widened, and I clammed right up. I looked again. His hair was dark, going gray at the temples, his face tanned, with wide, gray-blue eyes. Why so familiar?

"Michael Rohr," he said, walking toward me and offering to shake my hand. "I'm Phoenix's dad."

❧

We walked together along the ridge to Angel Rock.

"I thought you were in Germany," I said.

"I lived in Europe for ten years," Rohr admitted. "I came back when I heard the news about Phoenix."

"You didn't make it to the funeral."

"I missed it by a week. Picked up my ex-wife's email in an Internet café, came back as soon as I could."

"Brandon never mentioned that you were in town." I was wondering what good Michael Rohr thought he was doing, showing up after the event when he'd played no part in their family life for a decade. Most likely Brandon thought the same.

"Brandon doesn't like that I exist," Michael confirmed. "Ditto my ex-wife."

"What about Zak?"

"The kid's OK with me being around. He was too young to blame me for what happened—*when* it happened."

"Between you and Sharon?" I relaxed a little as we walked away from the ranch house and barn, though it freaked me out that what was familiar about Michael Rohr was that he was the double of Phoenix, thirty years on. I tensed again as it hit me hard that Phoenix would never get to his late forties, would always be young.

"Phoenix never talked about the divorce. I just knew you weren't around."

"The split wasn't pretty," he admitted. "There were other people involved. Their mom was pretty angry. Still is."

This part at least was true. Whenever I encounter Sharon Rohr she comes across as a bitter, worn-out woman—one of life's angry victims. And she definitely doesn't bond with me.

Under Angel Rock, Michael and I stopped and looked out toward Amos Peak.

"Is there something specific you want us to talk about?" I asked.

"They say you come out here a lot." He chewed the inside corner of his lip as he spoke so his words came out low and indistinct—another Phoenixism. And he left gaps in the conversation, just the same way.

"It was our favorite spot," I lied. "Anyhow, who's 'they'?"

"The guys in town. I hooked up a while back with Russell Bishop."

"You did?" This took me a while to process. Russell is Zoey's dad—*Herr Commandant*. "I didn't think he talked to anyone worth less than ten million dollars."

"We go way back to when we were kids. I grew up around these parts."

"You did?" I repeated.

"After I met Sharon, we moved to Cleveland for work. After the split, she ended up back here, I guess because this is where she has her roots."

There was a lot I still didn't know about the Rohr family, I realized.

"So Russell tells me you're good buddies with Zoey."

"The best."

"You helped her through a hard time. He also says you were dating my son."

I nodded.

"Can't talk about it, huh?"

I shook my head.

"Even after a year."

"*Less* than a year."

"*Almost* a year." With his hands in his pockets he stared at the distant mountains. "You know why I went to work in Germany? Because Sharon kept the kids away from me, wouldn't let me anywhere near them. I tried the legal route. I tried everything."

"So why move away?" If he wanted to see his kids so much, how come he went to live thousands of miles away?

"The problem got too big for me to solve. I had to turn my back, walk away."

A small light went on in my head. "Gotcha." Think Mom and Dad, recognize how little I'd seen my own father these last five years—he wrote me once to say it was too painful. I nodded and turned to walk back toward the SUV.

"So the rumors about this old place don't scare you?" Michael asked, nodding his head toward the barn and the ranch house. "It's a little creepy, don't you think?"

"Why did you decide to follow me?" I snapped.

"Just to ask how you're doing."

"No—really?" I attempted sarcasm. It failed.

"Sure. And I wanted to ask about you and my son. But I understand you're not ready."

I swallowed hard. OK, so this was Phoenix's father, but even he didn't have the right. "I won't ever be ready," I told him, dead set on walking away. Michael stopped me.

"I guess I knew that. But I had to try. There's a ten-year gap in my relationship with my son, and I'm determined to fill it with a few details."

"Sorry." This time I did set off toward the two vehicles parked along the ridge and felt Michael follow close behind. He took long strides and soon caught up.

"I have something for you," he said quietly.

An older man showed me a precious picture for the second time in twenty-four hours—this time it's Michael Rohr sliding a photograph from his pocket and holding it between trembling fingers. "Take it."

I held the color print—two boys in profile, one tall, the other shorter and holding a football to his chest, wearing an oversized team shirt and gazing up at the older figure, giving him total eye contact. Brandon, age maybe sixteen, is grinning down at kid brother Phoenix, age ten.

"Keep it," Michael told me.

I refused the offer. "No, it belongs with you," I whispered. But after that I decided to try to answer some of the questions.

"What was he like—my middle son?"

"He was beautiful."

"You loved him?"

"Totally."

"How was he with other kids?"

"Quiet. He preferred to be on the outside."

"A loner?"

"At first. He was new to the school. He felt like he didn't belong."

"But you liked that about him?"

I nodded. "He scared me a little. I thought maybe he would look down on me. It turned out he thought I was the moody one—until he got to know me."

Michael soaked up every word I said, almost holding his breath as if this would help him store the memories more clearly. "What was Phoenix's thing? What did he like to do?"

"He'd stopped playing football," I said with a smile as I studied the picture again—Phoenix wearing his dark hair short, with his little boy face, his skinny arms. "He liked listening to music, walking in the mountains, swimming in the lake."

His dad nodded as if this was enough and he couldn't

bear any more. He murmured thank you, slid the picture back into his pocket, then turned away.

"Thank *you*," I told him. I watched him open the door to his SUV. "Would you like me to talk to Brandon for you?" I asked suddenly.

Michael shook his head. "You wouldn't change his opinion of me, I can tell you that for sure."

"So will you stick around for Zak?"

"I don't know. Maybe." He was getting in the car, starting up the engine.

"Zak's in trouble with the school."

This was news to Michael. He turned down the corners of his mouth, narrowed his eyes. He glanced quickly at me then started to reverse out along the ridge. "I'll check that out. Thanks for talking to me."

"No problem." A heavy, sad feeling came over me as I watched him leave. Add one more name to the list of people wounded by Phoenix's passing. Someone like me, who didn't know how to move on.

✦

I had to be sure Michael Rohr was gone before I walked down into the valley, so I waited until the SUV had disappeared among the aspens and the sound of its engine had died.

Then I waited some more.

Doubts crept back into my mind, like wind rustling the aspen leaves, disturbing my purpose. Why did it have to be like this, I wondered. Why couldn't I run down the hill straight into Phoenix's arms, plain and simple?

Because this is the end game, Arizona's dry, dead voice inside my head reminded me. I looked up, expecting to see her face among the bright, fluttering leaves. *You do this for Phoenix, you solve his mystery, and you never see him again.*

Her voice became a sigh. It turned into a rustle of wind, a sound of wings beating, building, sweeping along the ridge, and swooping down the hillside.

Yes, this time I knew—the Beautiful Dead were back.

I walked—I didn't run. My legs felt wooden, my feet heavy as lead. Down in the valley the green grass rippled.

It was weird how dead spirits brought new life to this silent, deserted place. The wings beat and raised a wind strong enough to rattle the panes in the ranch house windows, to rock the truck on its rusting axle and blow wide open the old barn door.

I ignored the house and headed straight toward the barn, my feet still dragging, my heart thumping. I stood in the wide entrance, one trembling hand resting against the doorframe, waiting for my eyes to grow used to the gloom.

They were there, in their circle, turned in toward the center the way they'd been when I first saw them. But this time there were only four Beautiful Dead—Hunter, Iceman, Dean, and my wonderful Phoenix, emerging from the shadows as my eyes adjusted. They were all stripped to the waist, their skin pale and smooth, each bearing their death mark tattoo.

"Arizona! Summer!" I murmured. I longed to have them back, to see the soft faces of girls among the strong Beautiful Dead guys.

"We have come back from beyond the grave," they murmured in chorus as the beating wings stormed across the yard and seemed to drive me farther into the dark space of the barn.

The ritual was the way I remembered it—solemn and simple, recognizing their reason for being here.

"We are here to seek justice. It was a painful journey," Iceman said. "Hunter brought us back."

The overlord gazed at each in turn—first Iceman, then Dean, and finally my Phoenix, whose back was turned.

"He brought us here," Dean echoed.

"For one last time," Phoenix said. And now each of them reached out his right hand to meet the others in the center of the circle—four strong curled fists touching lightly, four spirits returned from limbo.

I was under their spell, watching with held breath, standing under a windstorm of beating wings.

"Phoenix, your time has come," Hunter murmured. "Darina is here."

❧❧

I'm in his arms, and it's real. His flesh is pale and cold against me—his cheeks, his lips. I feel his breath.

"God!" he murmurs, sinking his head against my shoulder. A tidal wave of relief hits me, and I drown. I close my eyes, stop breathing, hold on tight.

"I was scared we'd never do this ever again," Phoenix tells me, the words tumbling out. He's kissing me and talking, kissing me again.

I'm hanging on to him, dizzy and swaying. I can't talk. I can't believe it's happening at last. I look into his eyes.

❧❧

We sat together on the bank of the creek, Phoenix and me. The others left us alone, giving us the precious gift of time. I held his hand and felt his cold fingers wrap around mine as we watched the clear current swirl around granite boulders that sparkled in the sun.

I gazed at the water. *If I look at your face, you'll disappear.*

"I won't," he whispered. "Darina, look at me."

I turned my head. His fingers were still intertwined with mine, his eyes searching my face.

If I say anything, you'll vanish.

"I won't," he promised. "Darina, this is our time."

37

My fingers held on even tighter than before. "Stay with me."

"I'm here. This is the way it's meant to be." His voice was the same slow drawl, his eyes somewhere between gray and blue, the lashes long and curved, straight brows above.

"I waited forever. I came here so many times." My voice was quivery and small, my grasp full of fear.

"It's the way it's meant to be," he said again. "Believe me."

And then we were walking hand in hand away from the deserted house and barn, out through the meadow under a vast blue sky.

The crushing pressure around my heart was easing. I was loosening my grasp.

Phoenix smiled at me. "You came back."

"*You* came back!"

"I'm always here. I'm with you wherever you go."

I felt the sun warm my face, knew that his would always be cold as death. "I do see you here on the far side," I told him. "Maybe only for a moment, but I know you're here."

Phoenix, my beautiful Phoenix, nodded. And oh, my heart was racing, but not with terror. I smiled back.

"That's what I love—the way your eyes soften and melt."

He put his arms around me, lifted me clear of the rippling grass, and I felt the world tilt as I locked my arms around his neck and he laid me on the ground among the bright poppies, his body next to me, his lips on mine.

❧

"There's a thousand things I want to say and not enough time." We sat in the ranch house, face-to-face across the kitchen table. "When I'm home, I rehearse it all. I plan to tell you the things I remember best, how it felt the first time you talked to me, my fluttery heart, my head not believing what was happening."

Phoenix nodded. "All I could think was 'Dude, don't say anything stupid. Don't fall over or walk into the door.'"

"I was so scary?"

"It took me half a year to find the courage."

I closed my eyes and laughed. "Idiot." You can load any word you like with affection and it comes out like "I love you."

"You were so cool, Darina. You could look at a guy and destroy him—*zap*, he'd be gone."

"Not really."

"Yeah, you could. Girls like you don't know their power."

"Girls like me?"

"Beautiful and hostile—a killer combination."

"Listen." I reached for his hands. "That wasn't hostility— that was pure fear. Other girls—Jordan, Hannah—they're born with the confidence gene. They're out there saying 'Look at me!' knowing that the whole world adores them. Not me. There's not a grain of that anywhere in my entire body—I step out of my door each day armed and ready for attack."

"How did that happen?" Phoenix wondered, sitting in a shaft of sunlight that fell through the open door.

"It's not hard to work out. When my dad was around, he expected a lot. Always be good, be smart. And I tried real hard. Sometimes it worked—one time, when I was eight years old, I won a prize for making a speech in front of the whole school. Me! I was so chewed up with nerves I didn't eat for a week. Then there were times I tried to please him, and it didn't work. That's when Dad did a great job of ignoring me and making me feel like I didn't exist."

"Yeah, we have to please Daddy." Phoenix knew the score.

"That's the thing about fathers—you work and work at it then they leave home anyway." This was part of the bond between Phoenix and me, I realized. We were both abandoned kids. "I just talked with yours," I told him hesitantly.

"I know. Hunter was there."

Of course! "Michael needs closure," I told Phoenix. "He wanted to know about us, to understand. And he showed me a picture." Describing the photo of Brandon and Phoenix, I waited for his reaction.

Phoenix was silent, lost in his memories.

"What are you thinking?" I asked.

He glanced up at me then smiled sadly. There was a

lifetime of regret rolled up in that smile. "I'm thinking it was a long time ago."

❧

I already mentioned being unhappy with the fact that Hunter had returned with such a small group of Beautiful Dead.

"Where are the others? Where are Donna and Eve?" I asked Iceman after Dean had come into the kitchen to get Phoenix, and I'd found myself wandering aimlessly across the yard into the barn, where I found Iceman chopping logs.

"They didn't come back."

"I see that, but why? Where are they?"

Iceman let the heavy ax head swing to the ground, rested on the shaft, and shook his head. "Donna's twelve months were up."

Listening to Iceman's short answers, I struggled to picture Donna—always there but in the background.

It was her bright red hair that you noticed and that was all. I felt bad about not being more curious when I had the chance.

"Did Eve run out of time, too?"

"No. She found her answer."

Eve with her baby, Kori, whose golden hair shone like a halo.

Iceman read my mind. "Actually, Eve was here for Kori.

She needed to learn why her baby died. It turns out the hospital missed a diagnosis. Meningitis."

"And Eve?" I didn't want to hear that she'd lost her baby and died soon after of a broken heart.

"In childbirth," Iceman explained. "She stepped over six months before Kori. They're together now."

I let out a sigh then stood quietly while Iceman took up the ax again. I saw the shiny blade fall, heard the thud and crack as it split the log.

"It feels different without them, I know." Iceman paused again and spoke what I was thinking. "And without Jonas, Arizona, and Summer."

"They all left and won't come back." The barn was gloomy and cold, sad memories floated in the dust.

"And soon Phoenix," Iceman said, going back to his task.

"Iceman, I want you to stay here with Darina." Hunter strode into the barn while Dean and Phoenix waited in the yard. "Keep her hidden. If intruders come too close, you know what to do."

Intruders! I flipped into panic mode. "What happened? Did Michael Rohr follow me down here?"

Hunter had already turned away, but he paused to glance at me. "Not this time, Darina. No—Dean just spotted cops heading along the dirt road. It's Jardine and the new sheriff, coming to check the place out."

Knowing this had nothing to do with me, I relaxed.

Well, not relaxed exactly. Let's just say Hunter wouldn't be able to blame me for the new county sheriff driving out to Foxton. It was part of his job to check out the squatter rumors, simple as that. And Hunter's job was to protect the Beautiful Dead from intruders.

So I stayed in the barn with Iceman while the overlord took Dean and Phoenix up to the ridge.

"What will Hunter do?" I asked, climbing the crumbling wooden steps into the loft and finding a lookout spot between two warped planks. From there I could spy on the action up among the aspens.

"You mean, which of his superpowers will he bring into play?" Following me up the steps, Iceman leaned back against the rough wall, arms folded, not bothering to keep watch with me. "Don't hold your breath," he advised. "I bet Hunter will stand back and let the two visitors satisfy themselves that there's no cause for concern out here."

This seemed to be what was happening as I peered through my chink. I saw the three Beautiful Dead gather quietly in the shadow of the water tower. Hunter spoke a few words then surrounded them in a soft, shimmering light. I blinked, and they were gone. Superpower number one—the ability to dematerialize at will. But as far as I could tell from this distance, there was no calling up of the barrier of wings to stop the two cops in their tracks.

I waited a while, long enough to take in the trees lining the ridge—their slender, silvery trunks and bright canopy of leaves—and to think how peaceful and perfect this place was. Then two uniformed figures appeared.

They were two guys doing a job, probably enjoying the scenery like I did the first time I ever came here, with no clue what they might be walking into. One—the shorter, stockier one—I recognized as my buddy, Deputy Sheriff Henry Jardine, expert fly fisher and all-round good guy, the one who decided not to arrest Zak Rohr on a charge of arson. He was with his new boss, Danny Kors, and they were chatting as they strolled through the aspens, stopping after a while to direct their attention down into the valley.

"They've spotted the house!" I whispered to Iceman. "They're heading this way!"

Not strolling now, but picking up their pace, they kept their gaze fixed on the abandoned house and the heap of rusting parts that had once been a truck parked next to it, thinking maybe that the rumor was right—there were squatters here who needed to be checked out. Soon they drew near enough for me to pick out their high-alert expressions.

Right away I decided they fit the good-cop/bad-cop

formula; slightly overweight, kind uncle Jardine versus lean Mr. Mean Kors.

The sheriff made a beeline for the old house while Henry hung back to take note of a recent repair to the razor-wire fence in an otherwise neglected yard.

Inside the loft, I switched positions for a better view of Kors, who was stepping up onto the porch, testing the door in the kitchen then raising the sole of his boot to lash out and kick in the old lock. There was the sound of splintering wood then the door swung open.

I frowned, taking it as a personal insult that Kors was damaging Beautiful Dead property in the line of duty.

"Hunter should do something!"

"Sssh!" Iceman still wasn't looking, but he was listening hard. Superpower number two—they can hear a leaf fall from the distance of half a mile. He heard the door hinge creak then Kors's heavy footfall inside the house.

I kept my face close to the new gap, watching Jardine follow his boss into the house, waiting another few seconds before I hissed at Iceman, asking for an update.

"They're searching the place, currently heading upstairs," he reported.

Up to the one small bedroom whose window overlooked the yard, disturbing the silence of decades, flinging back the faded quilt, poking into dusty corners.

"Now they're coming back down."

I stared at the front door hanging crookedly from one hinge after the sheriff's forced entry. I thought of Hunter, Phoenix, and Dean keeping invisible watch.

"Kors wants to move on to the barn," Iceman told me. "Jardine is saying what's the point? Nobody's set foot in the place in years."

I saw the two men reappear in the doorway, Kors leading the way, stooping under the low doorframe as he stepped down into the yard. He stopped to stare at the moose antlers above the barn door, then, deciding to ignore his deputy's advice, he walked toward us.

Do something! was my silent message to Hunter.

Below us, I heard Kors slide the big metal bolt. "Henry, come over here!" he called.

"What did you see?"

More footsteps followed across the packed dirt surface. Jardine joined his boss.

"There—the ax leaning against the stall and the stack of split logs."

"Interesting." The deputy sheriff had evidently changed his mind.

We heard more footsteps, directly underneath. "And here—see the cell phone at the base of the steps."

My hand flew to my jeans pocket—there was no phone.

I sucked in air and felt my throat go dry. Iceman stood, watching me panic.

Down below I heard Kors place a foot on the bottom step.

My brain stopped working. I sprinted for the top of the stairs and, in my hurry to intercept the sheriff, I missed my footing and slid down the steps.

"Hey, where did you come from?" Kors grunted.

He lunged for my phone, but I scrabbled for it and grabbed it first.

Now, because of what I'd done, Hunter couldn't hang back. Straightaway he raised the winged barrier inside the barn, opened wide the door, and sucked in a thousand death-heads. Yellowing skulls with dark eye sockets whirled around us, pressed in, swerved away, whirled back again in the storm of wings to force Jardine and Kors back out into the yard.

I was fixed to the spot, holding my phone in the palm of my hand. Iceman stood at the top of the stairs, staring at me and shaking his head.

"Darina, come out here!" Hunter ordered.

3

Out in the yard I cowered under the beating wings. Their sound filled my head and drove me crazy—beating, beating, battering me until I dropped the phone and raised my hands to protect my head as I sank to the ground. "Phoenix!" I cried.

"He can't help you," Hunter warned, his voice ice-cold.

I collapsed, still shielding my head, curling up, waiting for the sound to fade, for the wind to stop, and the skulls to disappear. A few yards away, Kors struggled to his feet, dragging Jardine up with him.

"I'm sorry!" I told Hunter. "I shouldn't have done that."

"What's happening? Who are you talking to?" Kors tried to deflect the death-heads, using his forearm to shield his face and struggling against the beating wings, refusing to let the nightmare visions overwhelm him.

"No one!" I gasped. I'd never seen anyone fight back against the Beautiful Dead this way.

"You were planning to meet someone. Who was it?" Kors advanced toward me, through the wings and the skulls.

"No, I wasn't—I swear. There's no one here."

"What was that name you yelled out—Phoenix?"

I shook my head. Out of the corner of my eye I saw Dean take a silent order from Hunter then place himself between me and Kors. Invisible to the sheriff, Dean lashed out and upward with the back of his hand, making contact with the underside of Kors's chin and lifting him clean off his feet, flinging him backward until he crashed into Jardine. The two men fell to the ground. I heard Dean mutter something that sounded like, "Sorry about this, Henry," and I remembered again that Dean, the ex-cop, had once worked with my friend the deputy sheriff.

"Get them out of here," Hunter ordered roughly, keeping his steely gaze fixed on me as Dean, still invisible to his victims, raised them out of the dirt as if they weighed no more than rag dolls. They struggled helplessly in his grasp.

"Go ahead—you know what to do," the overlord muttered.

It was time for Dean to memory-zap the two guys. He threw them against the side of the house and sent some weird, superpowerful electrical current surging through their brains to wipe out all recollection of what had happened since they first set foot on Foxton Ridge.

I saw it happen—watched their bodies absorb the charge and twist in pain, saw their faces contort, their heads fall back and mouths open in silent agony. I groaned for them as their knees buckled and they finally sagged back to the ground.

And now, for the first time since the crisis began, I saw Phoenix—a blurred figure through the wild storm of skulls and beating wings—watching silently. I tried to run to him, longed to feel his strong arms around me, sheltering me from the storm.

"Phoenix, help me!" I whispered, though I absolutely knew he was in thrall to his overlord.

Phoenix, his expression fixed in an agony of helplessness, stayed where he was, close to the house with Iceman. I was still on my knees just outside the barn. Dean straddled the two semiconscious lawmen slumped in the dust.

Hunter, the puppet master, let the skull barrier fade then gave the silent order for Iceman to help Dean carry Kors and Jardine back to their car.

As the two men were raised from the ground and dragged away, I struggled to my feet and managed to look Hunter in the eye. Yes, I'd been stupid, I'd acted without thinking and caused a problem, but I wasn't going to cave in. I would try to stand up to him.

"When will you ever learn, Darina?" Hunter sighed.

He stood looking at the far horizon of jagged mountains then up at the clear blue sky, not expecting an answer.

"I said I was sorry. Anyway, Kors saw my phone—he already knew someone was here." Even though the wings and skulls had faded, my knees trembled and my voice was hardly more than a whisper.

"Not necessarily."

"He was about to climb the steps into the loft!"

"And you wouldn't have been there. I'd already told Iceman to get you out of there fast."

I gasped. "You ordered him to dematerialize me? How was I supposed to know? I'm not like you—I don't have telepathy."

Hunter finally turned his head and leveled his gaze on me. "You're *supposed* to take orders from me, end of story. You're not meant to think for yourself and make bad decisions."

Phoenix, I thought. *Step in here, stand up for me!*

"I can't do it—you know I can't," he whispered. Instead of backing me up, he retreated into the porch and watched from the shadows.

I had to plead for myself in front of the coldest of judges. "If Dean does his job, Kors and Jardine won't remember what happened out here. They'll go back to town and make a report—all quiet, just miles of pine forest and empty scrub, maybe the odd mule deer."

Hunter's eyelids flickered. "Likewise, Darina. Remember I could send you back in the same condition as those two, with a sore head and a big blank in your memory."

"I know it. And I know I can't stop you from doing that. But last night you saw how messed up my head's been lately, and you offered me the chance to walk away. Being here today is the hardest thing I ever had to do—seeing Phoenix again, loving him the way I do, knowing that this time I have to say good-bye."

Hunter's head dipped slightly—a nod of acknowledgment.

For once I'd got through the outer armor and decided to take a big risk.

"Think about what you told me last night. Imagine if you got the chance to be with Marie again—for one day, one hour, even a minute."

I saw pain then anger flash in Hunter's eyes. Phoenix saw it, too, and took a step down from the porch as if to protect me, before his overlord stopped him dead.

"Picture it," I went on. "Would you be thinking straight? No. One look at Marie and you'd fall apart. Don't tell me you wouldn't!"

"I would," he murmured.

I looked right at Hunter, opened my own heart, and put myself at his mercy.

"And still I'm here today. I came to save Phoenix."

❧

A plane traveled like a slow silver bullet across the vast blue sky. A wisp of white cloud tangled itself around Amos Peak.

The mountains were bruise blue in the late afternoon sun. Phoenix stood with me by my red car under the aspens.

"Hunter gave us thirty minutes," he said.

"Then what?"

"Then I have to go with Iceman to check out some kids over at Angel Rock."

"Kids," I echoed softly. Probably more far-siders made curious by the growing rumors about Foxton Ridge—it was a sunny afternoon, and they had nothing better to do.

"Darina, we need to talk," Phoenix began.

In my experience, that is never a good sentence. Guys usually follow with, "It's been great dating you, and I'd like for us to stay friends, but it's time to move on." For a split second I thought this was good-bye.

"No," he said quickly, tenderly. "That's not what I mean."

"What then? What's to talk about?"

"I want to explain to you what it's like for *me*, coming back to the far side, seeing you—how hard that is."

"I'm so sorry," I breathed. I realized that all I ever thought of these past few weeks was how bad it was for me—missing Phoenix, fearing that he would never come back to Foxton.

"Don't be sorry." Drawing me close and tilting my face up toward his, his lips brushed mine.

"All I want is for us to be together—you know that. It's all I ever wanted. Every time I step over, away from the far side, I ache for you. I try to picture where you are every minute of the day—what you're wearing, what you might be doing. I think of you and Zoey sitting together in class, of you and Hannah listening to Summer's songs…you and Christian playing guitar."

"That's pretty much how it is," I murmured, my lips against his cheek as I picked up another unspoken message behind his words. "You know you don't need to worry about me with Christian or Lucas or any of the other guys."

"It's not you I worry about. It's them."

"Explain."

"OK, so right now Lucas has Jordan, but Christian doesn't have a girlfriend. He's a good guy. Maybe he looks at you and thinks, 'It's been tough for Darina. I could step in and be her rock.'"

"Christian!" We were talking Christian Oldman—the boxer, the car fixer, the all-round guy's guy.

"It's not impossible."

"Yes—it is!" I smiled then kissed him again. "But thanks for being jealous!"

Phoenix closed his eyes for a while and seemed to relax. "I do know what I'm asking. Not even asking—just hoping."

"I don't want anyone except you," I promised. "You can stop thinking about it. Now, do you want us to discuss what Hunter asked me to do?"

Phoenix opened his eyes then shrugged.

"Hey, Mr. Casual, do you want to know or not? I'll tell you anyway. He said for me to drive back to town and talk to your mom."

He stared steadily into my eyes. "I already know."

"Yeah, of course." I keep forgetting—you get yourself a Beautiful Dead boyfriend and telepathy is part of the package. They're better at it than the brain scanners in any high-tech hospital, so you keep no secrets, whether you want to or not. "So Hunter said, talk to Sharon, ask her if the cops gave her more details about the way you died."

Phoenix was still gazing at me, tracking every minuscule neural connection in my brain.

"I know—you're thinking that's not as easy as it might sound, since I'm not at the top of your mom's list of favorite people."

"There's that to face," he agreed. "How come it's turned out that way?"

It was my turn to shrug. "It's like she's accusing me of something, and I don't exactly know what. She just doesn't like me, period." I thought again of the times I'd tried to help Zak and been on the end of Sharon Rohr's hard, ungrateful stare, of the dozen times she'd passed me by in the street.

Phoenix leaned against the side of my car, standing on one hip and kicking at loose stones with the free foot. "You have to understand, Mom never had things easy. She was young—just nineteen—when she married my dad. He promised a lot of stuff that he never delivered. Then he messed around with someone else, walked away, left her with three young kids."

"I understand. I really do. But I think it's more personal than that, more aimed directly at me. Maybe it's connected with Brandon giving me the car…"

A pause for breath gave Phoenix time to pull me toward him and kiss me. "Listen," I went on, "Hunter's right about this at least—if anyone knows more details, it's your mom. Are you OK for me to try and talk to her?"

"OK?" He looked unsure.

"What? Am I suddenly speaking a foreign language?"

This time Phoenix didn't smile. "Did you stop to think, it hurts Mom big-time whenever she sees you? You remind her—"

"Of you?"

Phoenix nodded. "She knows I totally gave myself to you. She felt squeezed out of the picture."

"I didn't aim to do that," I protested.

"It doesn't have to be planned. It's just what happens—any mother wants to hold on to her son."

"I guess." Feeling that we'd headed down a cul-de-sac, I changed direction. "You know what I often dream?" I asked.

He grinned. "You mean, the one where I didn't die and we're still together on the far side? Or the one where you believe we can cheat this twelve-month deadline and carry on the way we are forever?"

"That one." I nodded and twined my arms around him. "Why not? We could run away—right now. Why don't we?"

"You mean—drive in your red car, head west until we reach the ocean, live on a beach in California where no one can ever find us?" Phoenix put his arms around my waist and spoke softly into my ear, teasing and lulling me with the music of his voice.

"I'm not kidding," I protested. "What's to stop us from planning our escape?"

He pulled back and grew serious. "The world isn't big enough, Darina. We're in the you-can-run-but-you-can't-hide scenario. Twelve months is all I get, no matter what."

"We can't even try?" I murmured. In my dream, Phoenix and I always found a place where the overlord couldn't find us, where Phoenix cheated death and we were free.

He closed his eyes, drew a deep breath, then opened them again. "Don't tempt me. And don't think I wouldn't love to do it, because I would—more than anything, believe me."

Then, abruptly, he pointed along the ridge to where Dean was walking through the aspens toward us. "Our thirty minutes are up," he said.

As I drove the interstate from Foxton to Ellerton, I rehearsed what I would say to Sharon Rohr. *I want you to know that the new car was Brandon's idea—I never asked him for it. It's his way of keeping his promise to Phoenix that he would take care of me. And I hope you don't think I ever wanted to come between you and Phoenix when he was*...No, skip that. *Plus, I've heard there are a few issues with Zak lately—maybe if I saw him, he would relate to me.* Nope, too cheesy.

In fact, whatever I came up with, there were serious flaws, knowing as I did that Sharon would most likely answer the door, take one look at me, and close it in my face.

Was there another way? Did I have to drive straight to her town house in the row squeezed between the movie theater and the computer repair shop, or could I be more subtle—write her a note asking to meet up for coffee, or track down Zak and ask him to pass on a message?

Only ten days to go, I reminded myself as I drove between the sheer granite cliffs on either side of the highway, coming out of the mountains, through Centennial on the outskirts of town. Deciding in the end that the direct approach was best, I headed for the parking lot behind the movie theater. A big sci-fi action movie was showing, and a long line curled right around the back of the building and along one side of the parking lot, on the wasteland where they'd recently pulled down an old office block.

"Darina!" Zoey's voice called from the middle of the line, followed by a cheery hey and a hi from Jordan and Hannah. "Come to the movie with us! We tried you on your cell phone. Where've you been?"

"Hey. I've been busy." I smiled at Zoey—it was good to see her in town on a Tuesday afternoon, still too skinny for sure, but looking relaxed and, well, normal. And these days she was out of her wheelchair, walking with two sticks. "Sorry, I can't join you."

"Why, what's so important?" Hannah acted like she thought it would do me good to see a blockbuster movie. "Give yourself a break."

"Sorry, but no." I was ready to walk on across the parking lot, around the back of the Rohrs' house. The line edged forward.

"We can buy you a ticket," Jordan suggested. "Do whatever it is you need to do, then come join us."

"No, sorry." Now I really was turning my back and walking away, knowing they would stand in line analyzing what was still wrong with me and what they could do to fix me. "See you tomorrow," I told them.

I crossed the asphalt and turned the corner, taking a deep breath before I walked down the row then swung through the gate into Sharon Rohr's backyard.

I saw the metal bench where Phoenix and I used to sit on summer evenings, noticed that no one had bothered to weed the small patch of garden below the kitchen window.

The door stood open, and I could hear voices from inside the house—a man's and a woman's. Then Zak burst out of the door, threw me a quick glance, and hurried past without speaking.

"Hey," I said. But he still didn't stop. I went up three steps and raised my hand to knock.

"Which part of 'Please leave' don't you understand?" Sharon demanded.

A conversation was taking place out of sight, in the narrow front hallway. A stressed-out man's voice replied, "Sharon, I only want to…listen to me, please!"

"You think you can walk in here asking for Phoenix's stuff? No way."

"I know how you feel, I understand."

"No, Michael, you don't. Not the first thing. See—I'm picking up the phone, I'm calling the cops."

My hand was still raised, but when I heard the name *Michael* the knock didn't happen. Realizing that Phoenix's dad was the unwelcome visitor, I stayed where I was.

"All I want is to walk away with something that belonged to Phoenix," he muttered. "A shirt, a bag, a book, anything. Why is that such a big issue for you, Sharon?"

Personally I could see why—the guy cheats on her then disappears for almost ten years, he doesn't even make it to his son's funeral, and now he shows up on the doorstep, begging for mementos. Then again, I'd seen him in the flesh and knew what he was going through.

And he'd shown me the photograph.

There was a gasp of anger from Phoenix's mother.

I guess she threw something at her ex—maybe the phone. I heard it clatter to the floor.

"Michael, for years we had nothing—not even a phone number for you. So how in God's name could Phoenix call to tell you he made the school football team, or his best buddy was hurt in a car crash, or his big brother got sent to jail?" Sharon hurled a whole tidal wave of blame at her ex. "Did you ever once think about any of that? How a kid needs a father, and needs him most in the bad times. Did you ever think of me dealing with the kids by myself, Michael? I had no one to turn to when Brandon got caught fighting in the street over some stupid girl and they put him in reform school. His little brothers were scared that they'd lost him forever, just like they lost their dad. Soon Phoenix starts to follow in Brandon's footsteps." She paused for breath and for him to take in what she'd just said. "You want to know more about your golden boy? That's the main reason you're here, right?" I heard Michael give a stuttering reply that I couldn't make out.

"You think it's all good news?" Sharon challenged. "Poor, angelic dead boy who never put a foot wrong!"

Ouch! I flinched and almost turned and ran.

"No," he stammered. "I know it's not. I've asked people in the neighborhood. Phoenix was mixed up in things he shouldn't have been."

"Just like Brandon." Sharon's sigh turned into a sob that caught in her throat. "Those boys grew taller than me, Michael. I don't remember the exact time when I lost control, only one day I realized they didn't listen to me anymore. They went out nights instead of doing school-work, stayed out late, got into more fights."

Not true, not Phoenix! I wanted to step forward into the hallway to clean up Sharon's picture of her second son.

But I didn't because some kind of nasty curiosity had wormed itself to the front of my brain. What exactly was Phoenix supposed to be guilty of?

"It drove me crazy. That was why I moved the family back here to Ellerton—the boys were bad news up in Cleveland. Brandon was out of the correctional facility, but he couldn't find a job. Then the school called to tell me that Phoenix had lost his cool and punched another boy during a football game—they suspended him for half a semester."

"I'm sorry," Michael told her. "I wish I'd known."

"That is so feeble." She groaned, sighing again and stretching the four simple words for maximum effect. "You wish you'd known that you had two kids skidding off the rails so fast no one could catch them? And I had to stand by and watch it happen, not once but twice."

"What about Phoenix's girl?" Michael asked.

"Darina." A ton of scorn weighed down Sharon's next sentence. "You want to hear that your son was saved by love? Is that it?"

No! Now I really had to step forward and stop her, before she said something that scythed me down and left me dead.

"I already spoke with Darina out at Foxton," Michael told her. "We're a year on from Phoenix dying, and the poor kid is still grieving."

"I have news for you—Darina didn't save Phoenix," Sharon scoffed. She'd stopped her rant and had become cool and merciless. "You think she kept him focused on his schoolwork, away from the street gangs? Think again."

I love him. He loves me. That's enough.

"That's not how it worked," she explained to her ex. "You have to realize that Phoenix wasn't really in love with Darina—or at least not in a healthy way. It was more like an obsession. That was his personality—he had an addictive streak. He craved Darina like a drug. He couldn't be away from her for a single minute. He had to go wherever she went, do whatever she wanted him to do."

A jolt of surprise shot through me, and I shuddered.

Phoenix's dad tried to soften the picture. "That's what it's like when you're seventeen years old—remember?"

"No, Michael—you're not hearing me. Darina had a bad kind of power over your son."

"What do you mean?"

Sharon paused, preparing herself before she handed him some important facts. "Darina was waiting to meet Phoenix out at Deer Creek the night he got stabbed. He stopped at the gas station to buy gas, and he was in too big a hurry to get to Darina, so he edged a kid named Nathan out of the line. There was an argument. Brandon happened to be hanging out there with his buddies. He saw the fight flare up. He warned Phoenix not to overreact."

"Brandon says the fight was over Darina?"

I took a step forward, hesitated, felt the words hit like hammer blows.

"According to Brandon, Nathan told Phoenix that Darina would have to wait, that's all. Phoenix flipped. He punched Nathan right in the jaw, sent him sprawling against a gas pump."

"Other kids joined in?" Michael muttered.

"Nathan's brother, Oscar, was there. He stepped in to help his kid brother then Brandon moved in to take care of Phoenix. One thing led to another—punching, kicking, yelling. Then more of the older guys from out of town showed up on their Harleys. That's when the gas station manager called the cops."

"Who were these older guys? What did they have to do with anything?"

"They were the ones with the weapons," Sharon told Michael flatly, her voice fading to a whisper. "Oscar's buddies. One of them pulled a knife."

"I hear you," Michael said after a long pause. "They hunt in packs. Phoenix didn't stand a chance."

"And if Phoenix had just waited in line instead of fixating on meeting with Darina at Deer Creek, he'd still be alive today," Sharon said.

❧❧

My fault. Totally my fault.

Try telling me it wasn't, that no way did I plan for it to turn out the way it did. I won't hear you. I'll just remember what Sharon said. I'll recall standing by the creek that night, impatient, looking at my watch, thinking, Phoenix, where are you? *And I'll blame myself forever.*

❧❧

After Sharon said this and the guilt had time to hit, events moved fast. Footsteps came running down the alley, across the yard, and Zak and Brandon burst into the kitchen.

Zak must have warned his big brother that I was there, too—the second unwelcome guest along with their estranged dad—so Brandon didn't act surprised. Instead, he took hold of my wrist and dragged me through the house toward the hallway, where we found Sharon still trying to persuade Michael to leave.

It wasn't working—Michael was heading upstairs toward Phoenix's old bedroom, to grab the memento he'd come for. And it was ugly. Sharon had clutched her ex's foot and was using her full weight to drag him back. Michael was kicking out, but he had tipped forward and lay full length on the stairs. In one second, Brandon had leaped over his mother and taken hold of his dad from behind.

Michael was halfway up the stairs, trying to swing around to face Brandon, but he lost his balance a second time, and the two guys tumbled down into the hallway, where they wrestled on the floor.

Sharon yelled for them to stop then, seeing Zak, pushed him out of the way, back toward the kitchen. He crashed into me, leaving me in a heap on the floor while he sprang up and ran to wrench open a drawer by the sink.

Meanwhile Brandon and his dad were evenly matched—they rolled on the floor, grunting and swearing, Michael's arm locked around Brandon's throat as they thrashed against a flimsy hall table meant for keys and bags. The table went up in the air, making contact with the mirror above it, which fell down and splintered.

"Watch out—broken glass!" I warned. Already a cut on Michael's forearm had begun to bleed. "Make them stop!" I yelled at Sharon.

Then Zak reappeared, knife in hand.

I saw the blade, long and curved—a knife for carving meat. And the scary look in Zak's eyes.

Sharon wasn't looking at Zak. Her back was to him, and she was treading over shards of mirror, stooping to wrench Brandon away from his dad. "Someone will get killed!" she shrieked. Blood was streaming from Michael's arm; there was a cut on Brandon's jaw.

"Zak's got a knife!" I yelled.

Brandon and Michael looked up from the floor. Sharon spun around. Zak was walking down the hallway, wielding the carving knife in front of him like a sword, looking from me to his mom then down at his brother and dad.

We all stopped struggling, yelling, even breathing, and stared at Zak.

His eyes were wide; he drew jerky breaths.

Calmly Michael broke free of Brandon and stood up, blood dripping from his arm. He took two steps toward Zak. "Son, put the knife down."

Zak gasped, looked confused, glanced at the knife then dropped it like a hot coal. It clattered to the floor.

Sharon darted forward to pick it up. Silently Michael turned away, stepped past Brandon, and out of the front door.

I followed him. There was no point staying to explain. No point at all.

4

I was halfway across the cinema parking lot when Zak Rohr caught up with me. He came with a message from his mom.

"Tell Dad to stay away from the house," he warned.

"Mom means it about calling the cops. Next time she won't be fooling."

I didn't slow my pace, just kept on walking.

"You hear me?" Zak insisted. "You and Dad need to stay away from us!"

"Tell him yourself," I snapped. "I don't even know the guy!"

For a second Zak hesitated, giving me the chance to reach my car and open the door. But then he ran toward me and grabbed the door handle, resisting my attempt to slam it behind me.

I tugged hard and won the battle. With the door finally shut, I turned the ignition and was already moving off when Zak vaulted in beside me. He landed neatly in the passenger seat and grabbed the steering wheel. As the car veered toward a row of parked cars, I slammed on the brake and squealed to a halt a foot from the back of a Ford truck.

"Are you crazy?"

Zak kept his hand on the wheel, gripping it tight—the hand that two minutes earlier had been brandishing the knife. "Is that true? You didn't hook up with my dad?"

"I met him once—early today. That's it."

"So why visit the house with him?"

"That wasn't planned, it happened by chance. He and your mom were already fighting when I showed up, remember?"

It took a while, but gradually Zak realized I might be telling the truth so he relaxed his hold on my steering wheel. "So again—why the visit?"

"I wanted to talk to your mom about Phoenix," I admitted.

He shook his head, raising his hand like a traffic cop. "Uh-uh."

"Not a good idea?"

"Don't even go there."

For a while we sat in silence, the car slewed at an angle and looking like it had been abandoned between two neat rows. I realized that dusk was falling and was glad that the line for the movie had disappeared. At least Hannah, Zoey, and Jordan wouldn't be witnessing this. "Sharon blames me," I muttered. "I heard what she told Michael—if it wasn't for me, Phoenix would still be alive."

"She gave him the story about Phoenix running late?" Zak's eyes narrowed. His mood had altered suddenly, from crazy, out-of-control kid to been-there, got-the-T-shirt cynic. It made me look him in the face for the first time.

"She said that was how the fight started—Phoenix pushed a kid named Nathan out of the line at the gas station because he was in a hurry to see me. That was the flashpoint."

"The gospel according to Brandon," Zak muttered, opening the car door and putting one foot on the asphalt.

I grasped at a straw of hope. "You're saying it's not true?"

"I'm saying you don't listen to everything Brandon says." He was out of the car, flipping up the hood of his sweatshirt, shooting one last glance in my direction as if he almost took pity on me and wanted to make me feel better.

"Right. So what are *you* saying, Zak?"

"Maybe that wasn't exactly the way it was." His voice was hardly audible as he turned to walk away.

I jumped out and followed him, grabbed him by the arm. "And you know different? How come?"

"Because I was there," he admitted before he ran off. "I saw the whole thing—the start of the argument, who was there, who said stuff, who joined in…everything."

"You were there?" I called after him. "So you know how Phoenix died?"

My question hung heavy in the air as Zak sprinted

between the rows of cars. Somewhere way down on East Queen Street, an ambulance siren began to wail.

Ever since I first went out to Foxton and found the Beautiful Dead, some part of me has wished it could be over. For twelve whole months, I've fought for them with every atom of myself—for Jonas to be released and to give Zoey her life back, for Arizona and Raven, her damaged and gifted kid brother, for pure-hearted Summer who lived for music.

I do it—I rescue them and set them free, yet my heart doesn't beat smoothly. In my mouth I carry the taste of death and ashes.

In the end there's no one to turn to. I see myself walking a hard, straight road to nowhere. The trees are burned and black, the steep hills and rocky horizons are desolate.

"It's a dream," Phoenix whispers, and I wake. It was the middle of the night, my window was open, and the white curtains billowed toward us.

Phoenix lay down beside me. "There is no road. You're not alone."

For a while I said nothing. I thought back through the day just gone to the fight in Sharon's house, to the knife in Zak's hand, the broken mirror, and the blood running down Michael's arm.

I recalled the way Sharon had looked. In the street, in a room full of people, hers is not a face you would normally notice—she has small, tight features, her gray eyes are heavy lidded and guarded. But today in her hallway, she was different. Lit up by anger, with color in her thin cheeks, her jaw and mouth set in firm lines, she seemed stronger than her ex-husband and her two sons, for all their muscle.

"All her life, that's the way she's had to be." In the dark, lying beside me, Phoenix read my mind.

"It's no good—no way will she talk to me now." I sighed. "You should tell Hunter what happened. Tell him we have to think of another plan."

"He wants to know what Zak told you," Phoenix whispered.

I rolled and reached across him to turn on the lamp. The soft yellow light cast deep shadows across his pale, beautiful face. "Who did he send to spy on me this time?"

"Dean. He saw you and Zak leave the house, but he couldn't get close enough to hear."

Biting my bottom lip, I lay back against my pillow and stared up at the ceiling.

"Did Dean tell you how come Michael left the house covered in blood? How Brandon got the cut on his face? Did he tell you about Zak and the kitchen knife?"

This was all news to Phoenix. He put together the

pieces and jumped to the wrong conclusion. "You're saying that Zak—"

"No, don't panic. Michael and Brandon fought. They broke a mirror. There was glass everywhere."

He swallowed hard and sat up, swinging his legs over the side of the bed so that his back was to me.

"Darina, if you want to give up on me and my lousy family, I won't blame you."

I sat up beside him. "They don't do too much talking, do they?"

"The Rohrs have short fuses," he admitted. "No one stops to think."

"Or listen to what other people have to say. And I thought my family was bad that way." I turned to catch Phoenix in profile, head down.

"Some days it was like living in a war zone," he muttered. "First, when I was a little kid, my dad and mom were always fighting. Then it was Brandon and Mom. As soon as I grew old enough, age ten, I took every chance I could to walk out of there. I didn't care where, just so long as I didn't have to stay in the house."

Little lost kid roaming the streets. "Hey, look at me," I whispered. Phoenix didn't respond. "Look at me!"

Slowly he turned his head. "I guess Mom told Dad a lot of bad stuff, back at the house?"

I nodded. "She wanted to know where he was when Brandon went to the correctional facility, when you got suspended from school in Cleveland…"

"You heard it all?"

"It's OK. It doesn't make any difference to the way I feel."

"Sure?" There was a knot of doubt between his eyes, as if he was waiting for me to back off now that I knew the worst about him.

I studied his face. "Did you really punch a kid during a football game?"

Phoenix blinked, and the frown deepened. "Luke Missoni. He threw the first punch—from behind. I went down in the dirt, and while I was down, he kicked me in the ribs."

"They didn't see that?"

He shook his head and ran his hand through his hair. The stray lock at the front swung back across his forehead.

"Missoni lied about it later."

"I believe you." Relieved, I raised my hand and pushed the lock back again, deciding that this was the moment to release my guilt avalanche. "There's something else. Sharon told Michael that the fight at the gas station started because of me. You pushed into the line ahead of a kid named Nathan because you knew I was waiting at Deer Creek. You punched him in the jaw."

Tell me it isn't true. Let me off the hook. Give me another version that doesn't involve me, like the fight on the football field. But that would have been too easy—for Phoenix to have perfect recall of the events leading to his death. The fact that he couldn't was the whole reason we were here.

He looked down. "No way. Where did Mom get that idea?"

"Nice try." I sighed. I didn't have to be a mind reader to know he was lying. "You don't remember anything about the Nathan incident, do you?"

Shaking his head, Phoenix stood up and walked to the open window, where he gazed out at a black, cloudy sky. He seemed to be weary of a weight he carried, of the confusion, the fight, the blade, the blood.

"Something else I learned today," I went on. "Zak told me he was at the gas station with you that night."

Phoenix stood silently in the shadows.

"Was he? Do you remember that part?"

The answer, when it came, was slow and unsure. "Let me think it through. I guess I remember leaving the house. For some reason I was late—Mom wanted me to run an errand, she needed cash from the ATM machine. Then she said would I drive Zak to a buddy's house in Forest Lake? I didn't want to do that—I was already running late, plus I was out of gas."

"Keep going," I urged as Phoenix ground to a halt.

We were reaching the limit—soon everything would collapse into a huge black void. This happens with all the Beautiful Dead—when they get close to the point of dying, there's a big hole in their memory, as if the trauma of that sudden, violent moment of leaving this life turns their brain cells to mush. "Did you lose the argument with Sharon? Did Zak get in the car with you?"

He nodded. "I planned to get gas then drive him out to Forest Lake. Then it was back to Deer Creek to meet you."

"Gas first?" We needed to be clear. "So Zak *was* there."

"I guess."

"But you don't remember clearly? Listen, that's OK. We assume you two left the house together. But if Zak was there all along, why didn't he say so before now?"

"Because!" Phoenix said quietly.

"Keeping quiet was your mom's idea," I guessed. "She wanted to keep his name out of it. It was bad enough that Brandon was being interviewed by the cops."

Mother tiger protects her cubs. Quietly I went to stand beside him. We stared out of the window at the clouds drifting clear of the moon. "I'll talk to Zak again," I decided. "Somewhere, deep down, I get a feeling that he's on my side."

❧

Jacob Miller wasn't a kid you would normally want to

spend time with. As soon as he hit funky fourteen, he stopped washing and started shaving and piercing. He doesn't change his clothes more than once a month, and his hair is so short you can see every bump and dent in his Neanderthal skull. But the next day I went looking for him after school.

"Jacob, I need Zak Rohr's number," I began, skipping the "Hey, how're you doing?" and "Good, thanks" preliminaries. We were out in the schoolyard, close to the janitor's office, huddled under an awning because the clouds from last night still hung low over the mountains and had turned to slow rain.

Jacob stared at me like I was the one who'd crawled out from under a stone.

"Zak's number?" I said again.

You couldn't print his answer, only that it ended with the words cradle snatcher. A couple of kids from his class were standing nearby, and they let out croaky hyena laughs.

"OK, but this is important." I kept my voice steady. "When do they let him back in school?"

"Who's asking?" Jacob's little gang gathered around, fixing on me as the after-school entertainment. I saw his sidekick, Taylor Stafford, lurking in the background.

Remember—Taylor, Jacob, and Zak were involved together in the small matter of arson earlier in the year.

"*I'm* asking, Jacob. Now do me a favor, tell me where I can find Zak."

"That would be a no." Jacob grunted, sticking his fists deep in his low-slung jeans pockets.

"N-O, no," Taylor echoed, stepping forward and getting right in my face. Taylor is marginally less nasty than Jacob, but then that isn't too much of a stretch.

I refused to back off. "Where does Zak hang out? Are you going to tell me or do I waste my time hanging out on his street corner until he shows up?"

I got a second unprintable reply, then Zoey interrupted our cozy chat. I guess she thought, rightly, that I needed rescuing from this bunch of gorillas.

"Darina, you missed a great movie!" she breezed from the driver's seat of her shiny black SUV—a recent gift from her dad for coming through her surgeries and months of physical therapy. "Get in," she invited, leaning across to open the passenger door.

I didn't want to disappoint her. Besides, Zak's buddies were quickly sliding out of control with the abuse and physical intimidation. "Thanks." I sighed, sinking into the black leather seat.

"Do you have time to drive out to Turkey Shoot with me?"

"I have an hour." Glancing over my shoulder, I saw a single red rose wrapped in cellophane, resting on the backseat. Turkey Shoot Ridge was where Jonas crashed his Harley—a trip back there would be a pilgrimage for Zoey.

She nodded. "Good. We can talk while we drive."

Talking meant Zoey taking care of me, checking that I was doing OK as Phoenix's anniversary drew near. "You look wrecked," she began as we drove out through Centennial. "I guess you're not sleeping."

"Not a whole lot."

"Twelve months is coming up. Look at it one way, it feels like a lifetime. Look again, and it just happened yesterday."

"It hurts the same, if that's what you mean."

"I know. I still walk into school and expect to see Jonas sitting with Lucas and Christian. I swear he's there. Then I blink, and he's gone."

"I see Phoenix," I murmured. *Really, I do!*

"But somehow it's not hurting me anymore," Zoey explained, taking a turn down a quiet residential road. "I can drive this street where Jonas picked me up that day, and now I'm not in pain. Rather, I remember how sunny it was, how great he looked, how he smiled at me in that special way when he pulled up at the curb."

I told her I was glad to hear it. "Getting through the anniversary, watching the procession out of town to Turkey Shoot—was that tough for you?"

She thought a while. "I was really not expecting to get

through it like I did. But you recall what happened just before—when I was out in the stable yard that time with Merlin and Pepper, and I felt Jonas came to see me to tell me he was OK, that he loved me and I should live my life knowing that? It sounds weird now, doesn't it?"

"I remember," I murmured. "And no, it doesn't sound weird." If I'd done one wholly selfless thing this past year, it had been to argue with Hunter to let Beautiful Dead Jonas visit Zoey one last time.

"You have to know the same thing—that Phoenix totally loved you," Zoey confided.

He did, right from the start—I'm certain of that.

❦

In the beginning.

"You dropped this." Phoenix Rohr picks up my silver bracelet and hands it to me. His fingertips touch my palm. It's Hannah's sixteenth birthday party, at her big house next to the bank in the center of town. I've been hanging out with Logan, acting as if I don't need or like anyone in the whole universe. We're talking fifteen, sixteen months ago, when I was hyper-uncomfortable in my own skin, hiding behind the biggest new thing in fashion, hair, cosmetics.

"Thanks," I mumble, bending my head, struggling to refasten the bracelet.

"Let me," Phoenix offers.

83

I hold out my arm, watch his fingers deal with the delicate clasp. Honestly, it feels like an electric shock as he touches my wrist. He feels it, too, clips the tiny hook through the loop then quickly drops his hands to his sides, looking down and away.

"Thanks," I say again. I twist my wrist and shake the bracelet to check it's secure.

"Cool party," he says.

"Yeah."

"Looks like everyone made it."

"Except Christian. He's out at Foxton with his dad."

It feels like the lame conversation is about to die from lack of air. Inside I'm kicking myself for being so dumb. I mean, I've had Phoenix Rohr on my radar ever since he arrived at Ellerton High, he's so totally beautiful. Every day my eye secretly seeks him out at the end of corridors, across classrooms, at the mall, the movies, at coffee bars. Along with a hundred other girls.

"Phoenix—ask Darina to dance, why don't you!" Hannah yells across the room, above the music, loud enough for everyone to hear.

I see fear freeze his features, and I almost die. "Ignore her!" I mutter.

"I don't dance," he mumbles.

"Me neither."

"You want to get out of here?"

Surprise question—delayed response. Eventually I nod

and follow him out of the bright, noisy house onto the dark, silent street.

"Walk?" he asks.

So that's what we do, Phoenix and I, on that first night—we walk the streets of Ellerton.

At first we don't say a lot, but Phoenix takes my hand, glances at me, grins, walks on. My heart thumps in my chest, I can't believe what's happening. And it's weird; I remember so well the physical sensations—the first shock of his fingertips brushing my wrist, the surge of adrenaline when he held my hand, the coolness of the night air against my hot skin— without recalling exactly what we said. I remember shop windows brightly lit, dark avenues of trees, pools of lamplight. And the loveliness of Phoenix close up.

"I waited a long time to do this," he tells me at last, leaning in, tilting his head to one side, kissing me.

That first kiss, that soft, warm touch. Warm. Alive.

<hr>

Zoey and I were clear of the city streets, driving up the interstate into the mountains. "Come back to me, Darina," she urged. "Honestly, you're strong. You can get through this."

I leaned my head back against the headrest, watched the wiper blade swish to and fro. "I'll tell you one thing that really is weird, and that's the way our friendship has switched around. It used to be me comforting you."

Zoey smiled as she pulled up at the roadside shrine to Jonas—a small pile of faded roses and lilies. She turned and reached back to pick up her crimson rose, stepped out of the car, and placed Jonas's flower beside the others.

"That's what friends do," she replied. Soft rain fell on the rose. "You took care of me. Now I take care of you—simple."

❧

Half an hour later I pulled up outside Kim's office, guarding myself against the old temptation to sit in the oatmeal-colored chair and confess everything. *I'm over that*, I thought. *The Beautiful Dead are real. I want to spend every last moment I can with Phoenix.*

AM SEEING KIM, I texted Laura then turned off my phone.

I walked up the path lined with low, clipped hedges, through the glass doors into Kim's primrose yellow room.

I never met any professional as good at her job as Kim Reiss—not teachers, doctors, *anyone*. She sits in one chair, me opposite, with a low coffee table in between. Today there's a glass bowl filled with small rocks and pebbles on the table, obviously there for a reason. *Don't get me playing silly games*, I think sullenly.

Kim only smiles at me, and I'm clay in her hands. She can wipe away my suspicion and mold me any way she wants. "I want you to choose some stones," she explains. "Find one that fits your mood right now."

I'm feeling calm so I choose a smooth cream pebble. I weigh it in my palm.

"Now choose ones that fit other aspects of the way you feel. Tell me what they represent."

For a second I'm backing off again, telling myself no, I'm not playing. Then I glance up at her. She has clear gray eyes, a long face with a mysterious scar on her cheek, a mouth where a gentle smile hovers. I cave in. *OK. This tiny white stone is me when I'm scared, this sharp black lava stone is for when I'm angry and blaming myself, this crystal quartz with the light reflecting from it reminds me of Phoenix...*I set them in a row on the low table.

"Pick up the small white one," Kim tells me. "Describe it to me."

"It's me when I'm scared. You wouldn't notice that it has a hole right through the middle."

She looks at me, waits for more.

"I put it back in the bowl, and it easily gets lost."

"You think people don't see that you're frightened?"

I blink and look out of the window. "I don't let them."

"They see anyway," Kim says gently. Then she moves on to my big black guilt-and-anger stone.

❖

All of which leaves me feeling like I matter until I walk out to the parking lot and bump into Jim talking to Henry Jardine.

Jim's job is to sell and fix computers. He'd been working in an attorney's office next door to Kim. I just have to glimpse my stepdad for the big old black stone to come hurtling out.

"Are you checking up on me?" I muttered. "I already texted Laura to say I kept the appointment."

"How did it go?"

I shrugged then switched on the smile for the deputy sheriff. "Hey, how are you doing?"

"I'm good, thanks. I was telling Jim here about a fly-fishing contest in June. It so happens I'm carrying a spare entry form in my car."

While Jardine went off to get the form, I insisted on letting Jim know that my session with Kim was a success.

"We played with pebbles."

"Pebbles?"

"Yeah, and rocks." Let him think that Laura paid good money for preschool activities. The deputy sheriff was soon heading back with a sheet of paper, and I was already out of there.

"Darina, before you go, I want to give you and your dad the latest news on Foxton," Jardine said, real casual.

Ignoring the factual error over the relationship between me and Jim, I hit the mental brakes and slammed into reverse on my decision to leave. "What do you mean? What happened?"

"Hey, nothing exactly happened—not yet. But I'm letting people know that I drove out there with Sheriff Kors."

I tried hard to keep my voice steady. "You did?"

"You know how it is—they say a new broom sweeps clean, don't they? Danny is picking over recent big events in town, studying the deaths of the kids from Ellerton High. He's been listening to rumors about Foxton Ridge."

"Same old, same old," I muttered. I was expecting Beautiful Dead wings in the air above my head any time now—Hunter's way of warning me to take extreme care. "I guess you and Sheriff Kors came back empty-handed."

Jardine studied me closely. "Kind of. For some reason we both felt a little shook up afterward. It sure is pretty up there though."

"I like the place," I admitted. Jardine already knew I spent time on the ridge, so I wasn't giving anything away. So far, no wings—I must be doing OK.

"Laura and I wish Darina didn't visit," Jim butted in. "It's too far out of town. And they say it's haunted."

"They? Who's they?" I laughed.

"We didn't see any ghosts." Jardine seemed to agree with me, thank God. "It's kind of windy up there—you get weird weather. And those stories mess with your head if you let them."

"Not with mine," I insisted.

"Well, it's not just the rumors," Jim went on like a dog at a bone. "We worry there might be squatters—undesirables, lowlifes."

I glared at him. *Drop the topic!*

"No ghosts and no squatters either," Jardine reported. "We found campers down at the Government Bridge campground and a couple of hikers up by Angel Rock."

"Happy now?" I asked Jim.

"But I agree with your dad—it's not a place I'd be comfortable for any kid of mine to visit," the deputy sheriff added.

Thanks, Henry!

"It's too far off the beaten track, like you say, Jim. And, ghosts or no ghosts, it is kind of spooky. We didn't see any sign of civilization out there, but we thought we heard a door bang in the wind, maybe heard voices…"

"What did I tell you?" Jim crowed.

"We could've sworn we heard them," Jardine said, all the time keeping his eyes fixed on me. "I'm thinking maybe Danny will want to take another drive out there before too long."

I swallowed hard, said nothing. *Hunter, are you listening to this?*

"What do you think, Darina? Should the sheriff pay a second visit?"

"I really couldn't say."

"You never came across the voices, a door banging—nothing like that?"

"Nothing."

"No campers, no hunters holed up in an old shack hidden in the valley?"

"No."

Jardine nodded briefly then turned to Jim. "You want my advice? I'd say keep Darina away from the place—at least until Danny checks it out with the National Forest people."

"I hear you," Jim said.

Now I was out of there fast, heading for my car. These guys thought they had the right to restrict my movements. How old did they think I was, for Christ's sake?!

❧

One bad thing can lead to a good. I would never have headed for the mall if I hadn't have wanted to avoid the conversation at home with Laura and Jim, which would go like this:

Jim: Darina, take Henry Jardine's advice—stay away from Foxton!

Laura: You hear, Darina?

Jim: Answer your mom when she asks you a question.

Laura: Stay away from Foxton, please!

Jim: Else we'll take away your car keys. We'll ground you!

91

Not so much a conversation, more a set of orders shrieked into my ear.

So I cruised the parking lot at the mall to give them time to wind down after Jim's talk with Jardine.

And that's when I got lucky and ran into Jacob Miller a second time.

I saw him from a distance, climbing into the backseat of an old black Chevy. He didn't notice me, and the Chevy driver didn't give me more than a couple of seconds to identify the passenger sitting next to him in the front—a younger kid with light brown hair. I caught only the profile, but it was definitely enough to recognize Zak Rohr.

Of course I tailed them.

It's not easy to stay incognito in a car as bright red and shiny as mine. I had to hang back and hope the Chevy driver didn't check his overhead mirror too many times as he left the parking lot and headed out of town toward Forest Lake. Luckily it was rush hour, and there was plenty of traffic.

We drove for ten minutes, stopping at lights, cruising past the KFCs, Cracker Barrels, and Dunkin' Donuts lining the route. Then the Chevy turned off to the right into a district where old trailer homes were scattered among the pine trees and where broken trucks without wheels stood on piles of bricks and skinny dogs barked in dirt yards.

Great neighborhood, I thought, watching as the car I was tailing pulled up outside a derelict trailer and the four occupants stepped out. I decided to park out of sight a hundred yards back then approach on foot through some trees.

Up ahead I heard Taylor and Jacob telling Zak to relax and take it easy. "What's bugging you, dude?" Taylor wanted to know. "We've been here a hundred times. The place is a dump—no one has lived here in a long time."

"Yeah, I know." Zak seemed to hang back as the driver went ahead, carrying a blue sports bag into the trailer.

From behind a tree I spotted Zak still nervously checking things out.

"Zak, you want a beer?" Jacob called from inside.

Buying and consuming alcohol—not one of those kids was legal, except maybe the dark-haired driver, who looked twenty, maybe twenty-one. And I worried what else might be in that bag.

"Sure," Zak replied, finally following them inside.

I crept closer, only stopping when the car driver came back out carrying a can and a white plastic chair. He set down the chair and sat, legs sprawled wide, taking long swigs at his beer, giving me plenty of time to take in his round baby face, full lips, and stringy black hair.

Soon Taylor emerged, carrying a small plastic envelope. "Hey, Nathan, what's the street value on this?"

"Plenty." Baby Face was quick to take the packet from Taylor and stash it away in his pocket. "Listen, I only carry the stuff from point A to point B for my brother. I don't go into value."

"So how much does Oscar pay you?" Taylor sat on the trailer step, only to be shoved out of the way by Jacob, who threw an empty can down in the dirt and began to kick it around. Zak stayed inside—I could just make him out through the filthy window.

"Plenty," the driver, Nathan, said again.

Nathan. Finally the name got through to me. Nathan. The Chevy driver was *the* kid at *the* gas station on *the* night…

So it's a common name, but my gut feeling was that I wasn't mistaken.

And Oscar. You don't find too many Oscars in a town like Ellerton. The only one I knew was Oscar Thorne, the drug dealer who'd been sitting at a table near me in the coffee shop at the mall when my best friend Summer walked into a hail of bullets.

The driver of the Chevy was Nathan Thorne, Oscar's younger brother. And the white powder in the packet stuffed into his shirt pocket was a class A narcotic.

I must have been careless. The tree I hid behind left colorful bits of me in view—my blue patterned shirt, flashes of silver jewelry. Anyhow, Nathan Thorne suddenly spotted me. He stood up, tipping the chair against the trailer as I turned to run.

I sprinted back through the trees, skirting around low thornbushes, almost tripping, lunging forward, regaining my balance, and running on. Behind me, Nathan yelled at Jacob and Taylor to cut me off.

I could see my car parked on the road, maybe twenty yards away. Nathan was crashing through the undergrowth, gaining on me, and I felt the way a deer must feel with hunters in pursuit—heart pounding, lungs sucking in air, my whole system flooded with fear.

Taylor and Jacob had followed orders and cut down onto the road, planning to reach my car before I did. It was neck and neck. Ten more steps, and then five—I arrived with seconds to spare, turned on the engine, sped away, making zero to sixty in four seconds flat. If Taylor and Jacob hadn't thrown themselves sideways, I would have driven right through them.

I pointed my car for home and left them standing— Nathan, Jacob, and Taylor by the side of the road, Zak watching from among the pine trees.

5

Henry Jardine takes his job seriously. He truly cares about the Ellerton community and the people he serves.

That's the reason he was waiting for me at my house after he came off duty, long after it grew dark. He was out of his uniform, having coffee with Laura and Jim in the kitchen. When I came in, he stood up to greet me and take me out onto the porch.

"It's you I came to see," Henry insisted, sitting on the swing and looking up at me.

"Why? What did I do?"

"Relax. You're not in any trouble. I just know there's an issue between you and your folks, and it's been bothering me. I have a daughter your age, did you know?"

"No." Even though I was dead tired, I kept up my guard.

"She's at school in Forest Lake, thank God."

"Why thank God?"

He tapped the seat. "Sit, Darina. I do thank Him every day that Anya isn't a student at Ellerton High. Parents here—I can't even imagine the stress."

I sat down heavily then nodded.

"And you kids. After Jonas, Arizona, Summer, Phoenix—you all must get to wondering who's next."

"You missed out Logan," I reminded him. I don't often speak Logan's name because his dying and the way it happened hurts me almost as much as whenever I think about Phoenix.

"Yeah, Logan Lavelle. Add him to the list." Henry sighed. "What I'm saying, Darina, is that it might look like your folks are taking a tough line over Foxton, but you can see why they do."

"Yeah, and I need another lecture." I closed my eyes and set the swing in motion. "I don't know why you're all so hung up on that place."

"Are we? Yes, I guess we are. Including you, Darina. Weren't you up there when Logan had his accident? Yes, you were the one who drove him to the hospital. No need to say anything if that upsets you. But last fall, I hear you were on the ridge the day Arizona Taylor's grandmother fell from her horse. And there have been other times, too."

We swung slowly to and fro—the chains creaked. "So? I like it up there—away from…everything."

"And that's it? Because I wouldn't like to think you were getting sucked in by the rumors, that you go ghost hunting in that wilderness."

"Please!" Suddenly my brain clicked into overdrive. I opened my eyes and slammed my foot onto the boards to stop the swing. "If you really want to know, I drive out to Foxton for a school history project. I'm researching the old cattle ranches of Shepherd County."

"Cattle ranches," Jardine echoed, running a forefinger down his thick mustache.

"Before the National Forest bought up the land and planted trees, this county made money on the back of cattle grazing." Before I knew it, I was totally into my story, trying to convince Jardine that my interest in Foxton was legitimate.

"That's true," he agreed. "You wouldn't know this, but I'm ancient enough to remember the last ranchers. They were already old-timers when I knew them in the 1960s and '70s, with memories going back to the early 1900s. It was a tough life, bringing in steers from those mountains. The ranchers lived rough, rode all day, slept under the stars."

Satisfied with the way the conversation seemed to have drifted, I set my mind on quizzing Henry. "So there were ranch houses in the valleys back then?"

"Even as far out as Foxton Ridge. That's what I told Danny Kors the day I took him out there. Log cabins and shacks, probably gone now. Nature has a way of claiming back her territory, but maybe there are still a few old barns hidden among the trees."

"Did you ever hear of a rancher out at Foxton by the name of Hunter Lee?" I asked.

"Hunter Lee. You came across him in your research?"

"In the old newspaper archive. There was a report of a murder."

"Sure, it was big news way back then. Hunter and Marie Lee. Peter Mentone shot Hunter Lee dead."

"I read about it. They hanged Mentone."

As things turned out, Jardine was a local history nut himself. "There was a baby girl born later that year. The belief was that she was Mentone's daughter, though Marie went to an early grave denying it."

"Marie died?" I didn't even try to disguise the shock I felt.

"When the little girl, Hester, was ten years old. Afterward, Hester came to live here in town with her aunt, Marie's sister—a lady named Alice Harper, as I recall."

"And?"

"Alice Harper was a good woman. She raised Hester like she was her own, sent her to school then to college. Hester trained as a schoolteacher."

"Just like her mom," I said.

Jardine gave me one of his close, quizzing looks. "You

sure know your history," he muttered. "You're certain you never stumbled across any of those old ranch buildings out there by Angel Rock?"

"I've been looking, but I never saw any sign," I swore.

"When you do, remember to take photographs," the deputy sheriff told me. "Illustrations for your history project," he pointed out. "A photograph is as good as a thousand words any day."

❧

"You don't understand," I told Laura early Friday morning. For two nights I hadn't slept, and today I wasn't eating breakfast. All I could focus on was finding Zak again, until Laura opened the mail and dropped the latest bombshell.

"No way am I leaving Ellerton."

"The house is sold," she'd told me in a flat, final voice. There was a letter laid out on the table in front of her. "This is from the realtor. Finally, we found a buyer, but we have to vacate before the end of the month."

"You and Jim can leave. I stay."

"That's not how it works. You're still in school; you're my responsibility, remember?"

"I don't want to leave town. You can't make me."

"Darina…"

"You can't," I told her, getting up from the table. We were

six days from Phoenix's anniversary. This was the last thing I needed. "I want to stay here!"

What you want is not what you get. I ought to have learned that the day Phoenix died. The truth is, the more you want something, the more certain you are to lose it. It doesn't stop you from wanting it anyway.

Phoenix, stay with me, don't leave me here alone.

❦

Kim says it's how you deal with your loss that counts.

I hold the lumpy black lava stone in my trembling palm. "Anger," Kim says. "Deal with it. Who are you angry with?"

"Everyone. Myself. I'm angry with me. Phoenix wouldn't have gotten into a fight if it hadn't been for me." The stone is dark, rough, heavy.

"Lay it on the table, Darina," she tells me. "Look at it long and hard."

❦

Laura told me we were leaving Ellerton, and I stormed out of the house. I was halfway down the drive when suddenly my wave of anger crested, broke, and rippled onto the shore. I turned back. "Mom, I'm sorry!" I sobbed.

She stood waiting on the porch. She put her arms around me. "Baby!"

"It hurts so much I wish I could die!"

"Baby, baby, baby…"

Red-eyed and still shaky, I drove over to the Rohrs' house. Too bad if Sharon was there.

It turned out she wasn't, but Brandon was.

"Hey, Darina, it's been too long." He came out of the front door before I had a chance to knock.

I knew right away that he wasn't about to let me in, that the atmosphere in the Rohr house was at an all-time low. "That cut on your face—did you go to the hospital?"

Brandon fingered the strips of dressing on his jaw then took my elbow and steered me back onto the sidewalk, where his Dyna stood gleaming in the morning sun. "You want a ride?" he asked.

No wasn't an option, so I slid onto the passenger seat behind him. Soon we were cruising through the streets, downhill past the old psychiatric hospital and the Baptist church on the road to Deer Creek. When I realized where we were headed, I got ready to deal with a thousand Phoenix memories. Phoenix sitting on a rock watching the clear water whirl and ripple. Phoenix with his arm around my shoulder, wading into the creek. Phoenix with the wind lifting his hair back from his face, staring up at the mountains.

Brandon stopped right by the creek, overlooking a big smooth boulder in the middle of the stream—the exact spot where I'd waited for Phoenix the night he was killed.

Brandon cut the engine and sat in silence, legs still straddling his shiny silver and black machine.

"Why are we here?" I asked.

I'm waiting for Phoenix as the sun goes down. I wait a whole hour, playing a track from Summer's CD, wondering why he didn't at least take out his phone and call. The sky turns red then gray then black. Logan shows up in his white Honda, says, "There's a fight in town. A big one. Brandon's involved. So is Phoenix."

"It's almost a year," Brandon said, still staring at the clear water.

"Yeah." *Do I need you to tell me? Do I really?*

"Every day I wish I could turn back the clock."

I got off the bike and walked down to the water's edge. I remembered how we held the wake here, after the official funeral. Kids from Ellerton High decided to party, they said that's the way Phoenix would have wanted it—music in the open air, a celebration.

It angered me. Nobody understood what Phoenix would have wanted except maybe me.

After he died I'd seen him in school before I knew about the Beautiful Dead, then I saw Phoenix at his own funeral, smiling down on me in a halo of shimmering light. A glimpse and he was gone.

Now Brandon joined me by the creek. For a long time

after he said he wished he could turn back the clock, he didn't say anything.

"It's OK," I told him. "It's been a year. You can stop doing this."

He walked downstream. "Doing what?" he asked with his back turned.

"Taking care of me like Phoenix asked you to. You already kept your promise. Thanks."

"So now I walk away and you mess up?"

"What do you mean, I mess up?"

He walked a little farther. "You know what I mean. You see trouble, and you walk right into it. Take the other day—my family can't settle a dispute without you turning up."

"Hey, listen! Your dad came looking for me, not the other way around. Plus, I see why he needs something to remind him of Phoenix—I totally understand that."

"No, you don't." Brandon turned and strode back toward me. "How can you? You're not family."

I took a sharp breath and backed off. My foot slipped into the water.

He grabbed hold of my wrist and pulled me clear.

"I only want to help," I protested. "Let me, please!"

"Who do you want to help—my mom, Zak, me, my dad…or yourself?"

"I want to help Zak," I said, and I told him the latest

about his kid brother hanging out with Miller and Stafford, and the link with Nathan Thorne and drugs.

This is what makes guys back off from Brandon Rohr—the way he slams a steel door in your face. His eyes go blank. It's like there's no one home.

"Brandon, did you hear me? I said Zak is in trouble. Alcohol, drugs—it's all there."

He let go of my wrist and walked slowly up the bank toward his bike.

I ran after him. "This is serious. Are you listening to me? No way can Nathan Thorne be good news. He's Oscar's brother. You need to do something!"

Brandon swung his leg over the saddle and fired up the engine. "Didn't you pay attention to anything I said?" he muttered. "Family stuff stays with the family."

This was running away from me fast. "Don't shut me out," I pleaded. "What about the fact that Nathan was the guy who started the fight with Phoenix? You were there; that's what you told the cops."

He turned the bike around and pointed it toward the track.

I ran in front of him and grabbed the handlebars. "You said you didn't see who stabbed Phoenix, it all happened too fast. But I bet you have your own theory. You think it might be Nathan!"

Brandon stared at me with his dead eyes, then he swung

the handlebars out of my grasp. The engine roared, the tires kicked up dirt, and he was gone.

✦✦✦

I knew Phoenix was there, right beside me and invisible, on my long walk home.

"Were you down by the creek with me? Did you see how Brandon reacted?" I muttered.

Zoom—whoosh—zoom! A steady stream of traffic raced by, and my Beautiful Dead boyfriend stayed out of sight.

"How am I going to get the whole story if your family slams the door in my face? Nathan Thorne sure isn't the one to ask. And I don't want to mess with his big brother, either."

How many times do you see a crazy girl walking by the side of the highway, talking to herself? Car drivers slowed down to give me a hard stare then drive on.

"Plus, there's Zak," I told Phoenix.

I hear you, he said. *Let me think about it. Let me discuss it with Hunter.*

I stopped at the junction, swamped by a rising tide of frustration. "I wish we could go somewhere to talk properly."

Walk up the bank toward those trees, he told me.

He was already waiting for me in the shadows, with cars whizzing by below. He looked troubled and unsure. "It's a big ask—the whole story."

"I know it. But that's what we're doing, right?" Now

that I could see Phoenix, I felt my heart twist with pity. I longed to smooth away his frown, kiss him into a state of forgetting.

"Is it?" He drew a deep, shuddering breath. "I don't feel good about putting pressure on the people I love—my mom, Zak, and now my dad is here, too."

"I understand. But getting to the truth was always going to be hard—the way it was with Jonas, and with Arizona and Summer."

Phoenix gave a small shake of his head. "If it gets uglier—what then?"

I took both of his hands and made him look right at me. "Then we stand together and face it, you and I. We don't back off. We get there."

Slowly he nodded, his eyes locked on mine, his hands grasping mine. But a mist was surrounding him, a halo of light forming. He faded and was gone.

I felt a soft, warm wind in my face. It stayed with me all the way down the bank, along the road past the white church and the boarded-up hospital, along the streets leading to my house, then it disappeared.

I reached home at noon and found Laura's car parked on the drive when she should have been working.

"Where's your car?" she asked, back to old-style gestapo mom.

"Why aren't you at work?" I threw back. There was a pile of papers spread out on the table, and I'd noticed a stack of big cardboard boxes on the porch.

"Come and look," she invited. She showed me pictures of houses and details giving square footage, information on garages and basement space, bathrooms, views of the lake. "We're looking for a quick and easy move so it has to be a rental property. Jim visited two realtors' offices this morning, and they came up with these."

"It's still no," I insisted, pushing the papers away.

"How about this one in Forest Lake? It has lakeside views." She showed me a picture of a small gray house with a gable and a porch, pretty much a replica of the one we currently live in.

"Not even remotely interested."

"Forest Lake is only fifteen minutes from here. You could still drive into school."

Suddenly everything was different. "I'd stay as a student at Ellerton High?"

"If that's what you want," Laura offered.

"Yeah, it is."

"Then this is the right house for us."

❧

What did I care, so long as I got to keep my friends? I stayed to eat lunch with Laura then walked into town to pick up my car from outside the Rohrs' house, where luckily there was no sign of life.

For me, driving my car with the top down frees up my thinking, untangles the knots. *I need to be clear on my way through this mess,* I thought, stopping at a red light. *The only member of Phoenix's family who will even talk to me is Michael Rohr, and there's no point going there.* The light changed—green for go. I cruised on, out of town, following the route Brandon and I had taken earlier in the day. *Then there're the cops. Hunter told me that Dean was able to check out some files on the killing—the official investigation didn't find a weapon, and there were no named suspects.* For me that looked like another blind alley, though the new sheriff was back on the case, digging the dirt about Foxton.

Maybe he would turn up something new.

Coming out of town and heading for the open road, I passed the gas station. *Why don't you check out the scene of the crime?* a familiar voice inside my head suddenly suggested.

I braked hard. "Arizona?"

Concentrate on your driving. Take a left into the service station. Try to pick up a new lead.

I signaled, mistimed my turn, and cut across an oncoming driver. There was a squeal of tires followed by a blast from his horn.

Jeez, Darina! said Arizona-in-my-head.

"I know. My nerves are shredded. Anyway, you're not even supposed to be here on the far side!"

I'm not. You're hearing imaginary voices, going seriously crazy like everyone says.

I pulled up on the oil-stained asphalt in front of the gas station. "This had better be good," I grumbled, getting out of the car and walking right into an example of what the media would call compassion fatigue.

❦

The name on the gas station cashier's plastic badge read *Kyra*. She glanced up at me from behind her display of gum and chocolate bars. "Gas?" she asked.

I picked up a packet of gum then dug in my pocket for change. "No, just this, thanks."

Kyra went back to reading her magazine as she held out her hand for the coins. She had black, beehived hair, Cleopatra eyes, French-manicured nails, and an expression that said *I hate my job*.

"Can I ask you something?" I said. "Were you working here the night my boyfriend got stabbed?"

The question broke her off from her astrological chart for a whole two seconds. "You're the girlfriend?"

"Yeah. I got here too late."

"Now I remember." Kyra went back to her magazine.

"You were the person who called the cops?"

"That was me."

"You saw what happened?"

Sighing, she folded down the corner of her page and closed the mag. "Honey, I already answered questions from the cops, the TV, the newspapers, a million rubberneckers—they were crawling all over this joint. What's left to say?"

"Could you just go through it one more time?" I pleaded.

"Somebody, give me a dollar bill for every time I tell this story." She sighed as she looked me up and down.

"Please. It'd mean a lot."

"You're really young." She sighed, softening at last. "I guess Phoenix was, too. What was he—nineteen?"

"Eighteen, a year older than me."

"I never knew him before this happened, though I went to school with some of the older guys—Vince Hall, Oscar Thorne, Robert Black."

"They were there, right? That's why you called the cops."

"Yeah, the late arrivals were bad news." Kyra finally got over her fatigue and was warming up. "The place was already a mess—kids had overturned trash cans, there were hoses spilling gas everywhere. Those punks were wild. But Vince Hall and his buddies put the thing into a different league."

"Scary." I shuddered.

She nodded. "You get five or six guys in leather jackets riding up on serious Harleys, you know you're in trouble."

Soaking up every detail, I tried to steer Kyra toward my main question, *Who killed Phoenix?* "Up till then no one got hurt?"

"No, but those kids sure did a great job of wrecking the place."

"And how did the whole thing start?"

"Wouldn't you and everyone on the planet like to know?"

"Did you get it on the security camera?"

Kyra shook her head. "The camera ran out of tape two days earlier. I informed my boss, but he let it slide. And that night I was here in the office doing my job, so I didn't see the fight break out. The first I knew, seven or eight kids were throwing punches, bouncing one another off car hoods, throwing stuff around."

"And one of them was Phoenix?"

"Actually, no," she said. "He drove a black truck, right? And the way I remember it, he was standing by his truck, having an intense conversation with a kid in a black Chevy."

"What did the Chevy driver look like?" I double-checked my facts.

"Round face, long hair. Dark."

"Nathan Thorne. Let me get this straight—Nathan and Phoenix were talking, but they weren't fighting?"

"Not when I saw them. I didn't pay too much attention.

I was speaking to my boss on the phone, and he was saying call the cops. Then Oscar and Vince plus the rest joined in, and it was World War Three."

I needed time to think this through while Kyra took care of a customer. When she was done, I was ready with my next question. "So you know that Brandon Rohr was there, too?"

"Yeah, I noticed him. What's not to notice?"

"He's hard to overlook," I agreed, offering her a piece of gum. "According to Brandon, it was Nathan and Phoenix who started the fight."

She took the gum and slid it into her mouth. "No way," she insisted. "Those two were still talking way after the first punk threw a punch. Then the big guys joined in, and that's the point when Nathan got involved. I guess he had something to prove, but in my opinion, he should've picked on someone in his own league."

"So who did he pick on?" I asked as steadily as I could.

"Nathan Thorne took a piece of steel pipe from the trunk of his Chevy," my new star witness told me. "The guy he hit was Brandon Rohr. I swear to God, he laid him out flat."

❧

Deer Creek drew me back. It was noon. I was feeling a million miles from Phoenix and even further from solving the mystery of how he died. So I went to the place we knew best.

I played Summer's songs as I drove, sad songs like "Without You," "Invisible," and "Red Sky." *Red sky when I say good-bye, red sky makes me cry forever…*Crimson was the color of the clouds over Amos Peak while I waited for Phoenix that last time.

My life splits into three, and the sections don't overlap: Before Phoenix, During Phoenix, After Phoenix.

Before Phoenix—I was a normal kid whose main skill was in the superbendy department. Double-jointed is a bit freaky. It gets you noticed. Plus, it puts you at the top of the gymnastics league for under tens. Gymnastics, ballet, and a tiny budding talent for playing guitar. A major talent for misbehaving after my dad left home.

During Phoenix—a blur of ecstasy and open air, summer kisses. This beautiful guy loved me. For two and a half months, I held my breath and prayed it would last.

After Phoenix—I was all pain and emptiness. Another blur, nothing is real. Friends and family try to help, but they can't. I push them away. The closest I come to being able to describe it for Kim and once for Zoey, because she went through it with Jonas, is the sensation of losing my balance and falling down a dark hole that has no bottom and the sides are so smooth there's nothing to catch onto.

After Phoenix I fell and fell into blackness.

And then I drove out to Foxton and found the Beautiful Dead.

Today, at Deer Creek, the sky was intense blue and clear. The sun was at its highest point, the granite rocks sparkling pink and gray. I picked some white flowers, stepped down the steep bank, took off my shoes, and held up the light fabric of my white dress as I waded into the clear, cold water. I climbed onto the boulder in the middle of the stream and perched there, my knees drawn up under my chin, my arms clasped around my legs.

"Hey, Darina," Phoenix whispered. "You've been busy."

"Back again?" I turned my head sideways and smiled at him.

He sat in a glow of white light next to me on our favorite rock, legs dangling over the edge, dark hair lifted back from his face by the breeze. He wore jeans but no shirt or shoes. "I've been talking with Hunter and working stuff out." He sighed. "I still think this whole situation sucks."

"Don't talk about it." Turning toward him, I knelt up and edged in closer, wrapping my arms around him, feeling the cold smoothness of his skin. The softness of his lips made me melt.

The creek ran and gurgled, swirled and eddied, the sun beat down.

Phoenix kissed me for a long time, one hand stroking my

face and neck. I ran my fingertips down his back, tracing the angle of his shoulder blade, imagining the small death mark tattoo.

"What will I do without you?" I whispered at last.

He leaned away from me, looking at me through half-closed eyes.

"You know I want to go with you." I sighed.

"You can't. You have to carry on."

"I don't know how."

"We've talked about it. You go on, live your life. I'm always with you."

"If we can't cheat this destiny thing, and I agree we can't—won't you take me with you instead?" I would go with Phoenix wherever the Beautiful Dead went when their time was up.

"You know I can't. It's hard. Don't make it even harder, please."

"You won't take me?"

He shook his head, taking the soft fabric of my sleeve between his fingers. "I love you with all my heart, Darina. You know how that feels? It's total, and it's overwhelming. I'm lost in my love for you."

I kissed him and wanted it to last forever.

After a lifetime, Phoenix pulled away. "I want you to promise that afterward, when I'm gone, you'll still come here and talk to me."

"I promise." My voice was a sigh, a whisper, a sound like leaves rustling in the breeze.

"Here, on this rock. You'll talk to me, and I will hear."

"Will I hear *you?*"

"If you believe. And if you want to enough."

I will hear his voice in the running water, in the wind from the mountains, in the rustle of the grass in the meadows. I'll remember the low, slow sound of his voice and the soft touch of his lips.

"Hey," I said at last, tearing myself away and refocusing. "And I thought *my* family had problems."

"Enough kissing?" he asked.

"No way." I leaned in again with a small, tender brush of my lips against his. "But we should talk. I just learned some new information. Do you know Robert Black and Vince Hall?"

Phoenix thought a while. "Vince hangs out with Oscar Thorne."

"Right. Likewise, Robert Black. The gas station cashier identified them, said they were bad news when they showed up that night. I guess the cops interviewed them, along with twenty others."

"These two—they would come up with a story and stick to it."

"And the other witnesses, the younger kids—they wouldn't risk stepping on the big guy's toes?"

"That's the way it works," Phoenix agreed. "Brandon was always totally clear—you don't mess with drug runners and their gangs."

"Which leads me to ask why Brandon lied to the cops," I said, not fully prepared for Phoenix's reaction.

He leaned right away from me and launched himself from the rock, striding through the water toward the far bank then staring up at the mountains. "This is what I meant earlier—the thing gets uglier, the more stones you turn."

"It's true, Brandon did lie," I insisted, following slowly. "He told them the fight started between you and Nathan."

"And?"

"That's wrong. I spoke to the girl at the cash desk. She says what happened was that the guy Nathan actually hit was Brandon, and it came much later."

Phoenix still stood with his back to me, helplessly shaking his head.

I went back to my favorite theory emerging out of the witnesses' accounts. "OK, so is there a strong reason Brandon would want to highlight Nathan's role? Might he want the cops to pay particular attention because he believes Nathan's the one?"

"You're saying he's the kid who stabbed me?" For a while Phoenix seemed lost in thought.

"What's going on in there?" I asked, running my fingers

along his forehead and wishing, not for the first time, that I possessed the mind-reading powers of the Beautiful Dead.

"I'm thinking that's really going to make Brandon popular with Oscar—him putting Thorne's kid brother in the frame."

"Only if Oscar finds out what Brandon told the cops," I pointed out.

Finally Phoenix turned right around to face me. "Darina, there's a lot of hidden dynamics here that we don't get—gang stuff connected with drug deals. Ever since I came to Ellerton, everyone I met says Thorne has been mixed up in that." Looking deep into my eyes, he made a direct plea. "Take some time, step back a little, huh?"

Straightaway I hated this idea. "What does Hunter say about it?"

"What he always says—don't take any risk that would draw attention to the Beautiful Dead."

"But we need the truth!" I protested. "Am I the only one who sees how fast time is running out?"

Phoenix took a second to break through my frustration and sift through the whirlwind of suspicions and theories in my head. Then he took my hand and did his best to convince me. "Step back," he insisted. "Go talk to Jardine, share your new thoughts with him."

I saw the soft halo of light gather around him, knew that

he was about to leave again. "What about you?" I gasped. "What will you do?"

"I'll tell Hunter this is too big for you to deal with alone."

Phoenix's image grew faint. I heard his voice linger after he faded from sight. "Hunter has to keep you safe, I don't care what it takes."

6

That night and all through the weekend I did my best to put Phoenix's doubts out of my mind. *Hunter can't stop me now, even if he tried*, I told myself, staring up at my bedroom ceiling. *Hunter can't stop me now*. It became my mantra as each day the gray dawn light crept into my room.

Call me paranoid, or maybe it was lack of sleep, but come Monday, as I drove the streets trying to gather my courage and focus on my next move, I felt sure I was being followed by two guys on Harleys.

They came out of the Honda showroom on the edge of town and tailed me toward the mall, one wearing a red bandana, the other a blue, both wearing silver-rimmed shades and leather vests over white T-shirts.

I checked out these two Harley stereotypes in my rear-view mirror then headed on past the mall. The riders were still a hundred yards behind me, two abreast, so I built a scenario around the probability that it was already too late to step back as Phoenix had suggested.

Here's my theory: obviously Oscar Thorne had put two of his guys onto me. They had probably been on my tail for a while, seen me talking to Kyra, paid her a visit after I left, and learned that I was asking awkward questions about the Phoenix killing. They'd reported back to Thorne, who told them to tail me and stick with me.

Why would Thorne want to have you followed in the first place? I asked myself.

Because Nathan made a point of telling his big brother that you were spying on him out at the old trailer park. Go figure.

My pulse raced. It took two seconds flat for me to decide that dealing with me was now at the top of Oscar Thorne's to-do list and that I had to lose the guys on the Harleys.

Turning off the street into a McDonald's parking lot, I wove between cars, around the back of the building into a Blockbuster outlet, and out onto a narrow side street, heading toward Ellerton High.

Good job! A glance in my mirror told me that I'd succeeded in shaking the guys off. Still, my heart was thudding. I'd lost them, but for how long? Out of sheer habit, I signaled and turned into the school grounds, where I found Christian and Lucas standing by the entrance to the science and technology block.

"Too bad, Darina—you missed a fascinating lecture on

global warming," Lucas told me in that new, witty way he'd developed lately. "Jordan bought the whole package. She's busy reducing her carbon footprint as we speak."

I leaned out of the car, craving a little normal conversation. "How exactly?"

Christian pointed across the car park toward Jordan's bright yellow Beetle. "She ditched the car and walked into town with Hannah and Zoey."

"Where they have an instant relapse and start shopping for fashion items made in Asian sweatshops and jetted across continents for sale in air-conditioned malls." Lucas laughed and moved on swiftly. "Hey, Darina, I hear you ran into Michael Rohr a little while back?"

"So?" I snapped.

"Whoa, sorry. I didn't realize."

"What didn't you realize, Lucas?"

"That you'd bite my head off if I so much as mentioned the guy's name."

I closed my eyes and took a breath. "No, it's me. I'm the one who's sorry. So what about Michael?"

"Everyone's talking about it," Christian told me. "He and Brandon got into a fight."

Was that all? I thought that for once the Ellerton gossip machine was slow to catch up. "Yeah, at the Rohrs' place. I already know that." I sighed.

"*Another* fight," Christian explained, watching me carefully. "It happened early this morning, outside Zoey's house."

"Wait!" I cried, suddenly paying attention. "What was Brandon doing at the Bishops' place?"

"Not Brandon—Michael." It was Lucas who finally put the pieces together for me. "You know Russell Bishop is Michael's buddy from way back? Michael called to ask Russell to play a game of golf. When he came out of the house, Brandon was waiting for him. They exchanged insults, and it developed from there."

"And Zoey saw it all?"

"Right." Christian stepped back in. "She says it was her mom who called the cops."

"They called the cops?" I echo-groaned. "As if the family isn't in enough trouble already."

"The cops broke up the fight and hauled Brandon into the sheriff's office." Too late Christian realized the reason I was taking the news so badly. "Sorry. The Rohrs—a sensitive issue."

"It's cool. Thanks for telling me. Does anyone know what's happened to Brandon now?"

Lucas and Christian shook their heads. "I guess the cops will charge him," Lucas suggested.

"Maybe I'll check it out." Getting ready to leave, I made a feeble effort to lighten the mood. "Tell Jordan tomorrow is the day I lighten my carbon footprint, OK?" I pressed the gas pedal and swooped around in a wide circle to point toward the exit. "Today I have people I need to see!"

❧

"Sorry, Darina, Zoey isn't home," Helena Bishop told me.

I'd driven straight to the Bishops' home, knowing for a fact that Zoey was happily shopping in town. I'd parked outside the big gates and walked up the drive, stepped between the white pillars up into the wide marble-tiled porch, and rung the doorbell. "Actually, Mrs. Bishop, I only wanted a small piece of information about Michael Rohr, and I thought maybe you could help."

"You heard about the fight earlier?" she said cautiously. "News gets around."

"The whole town knows—you know how it is. I was kind of worried about Michael." I was glad to be talking to Zoey's mom and not her dad, who always treated me like public enemy number one. "I hope he didn't get badly hurt."

"I understand. Michael is Phoenix's dad, after all."

"Yes. I need to know his address so I can send a card, maybe some flowers."

"But he wasn't seriously injured, you know. The sheriff acted before things got out of hand."

"Even so," I insisted. "A card, telling him I hope he's OK."

Helena Bishop thought about it then decided to humor me. "That's nice of you, Darina. Wait here while I look up the address in Russell's address book."

While I waited I wondered how come life had lifted Russell Bishop clean over from Michael Rohr's rough side of the tracks to this land of smooth lawns and white pillars. Then Mrs. Bishop came back and handed me a slip of paper with a handwritten address.

"Thanks," I told her. I read the address as I walked down the drive—Apartment 209, Center Point.

The oldest tower block in town was where I was headed now.

Go talk to Jardine! I heard Phoenix's voice, sensed his presence in the car beside me, though he didn't actually materialize.

"Not right now," I told him. "I want to find out why your dad argued with your brother again. It might be important."

Step back! he warned. *Remember what we discussed!*

"I don't recall any discussion. The way I see it, you gave me some advice, and I'm choosing not to take it."

For your own safety, he reminded me. *This Oscar Thorne connection scares the hell out of me, Darina. He already put two guys on your tail.*

"Yeah, and I easily shook them off, didn't I? Don't worry. I can take care of myself."

Why aren't you listening to me? I'm telling you this is too complicated, too dangerous.

I sighed as I drove into the center of town. "This is weird. Why are you telling me to stop when we have only four days left?"

I pulled up outside Center Point, and a wind blew across the parking lot, lifting an empty white plastic bag into the air and whirling it against my windshield. It slid up and over my head, floated heavenward into a pure blue sky.

"Phoenix, are you still there?"

I'm always here.

"Have I got this right? Am I having a fight with my invisible Beautiful Dead boyfriend?"

Totally.

"So listen. You can't make me step back now. Not even Hunter can do that. I'm in this until the end."

There was a long silence before he sighed and said, *I know, but I'm scared for you. I love you.*

"I love you, too. Phoenix, you have to let me do this for you."

Silence again. A blast of cold air, as if Hunter had swept down from Foxton Ridge and pulled Phoenix right out of there.

Stepping out of the car into the wind, I pulled my jacket across my chest and walked quickly toward the building.

Rereading the address, apartment 209, I chose the second story, pressed the button, and waited for the elevator door to slide open. Its metal walls were scratched, scrawled, scribbled, and sprayed, its floor speckled with flattened gray blobs of gum. I ascended alone with a nasty smell and a fast-beating heart, stepped out onto a balcony, and followed door numbers 201 and 203 along the corridor until I came to 209.

I rang the doorbell, rehearsing my introductory sentences as I waited for Michael to answer it. "It's me again," I would say. "I need to know what happened to Brandon after the fight you two had. I have to talk to him. It's important."

Michael opened the door into a narrow hallway with a small kitchen on the left and a living room straight ahead. "Darina, come in," he said before I could speak.

He had a cut over his right eye and a livid bruise across his cheekbone. The eyelid was swollen, the eye almost closed. "Before you ask, I told the cops I don't plan to press charges."

"Good." I nodded.

"This was a family dispute. They promise to release Brandon just as soon as they finalize the paperwork."

I nodded again and followed him into the living room. I call it "living" room, but it was more an empty space for

Michael to dump his property, which consisted of a zipper bag stuffed with clothes and basic toiletries.

Otherwise, there was one brown velour chair, a coffee table with car keys and an opened can of beer on it, and in one corner a lamp without a shade. "What did you two fight about?" I asked.

"Let's just say unfinished business."

"And you're certain the cops will let him go? Because I need to talk to him."

"About Zak?"

"Kind of. Actually yes. I want to warn him that Zak's hanging out with the wrong guys." Which was true, but not the whole truth.

Wearily Michael ran a hand over his face. "You're too late," he mumbled. "Brandon already has all the facts. I picked up rumors from Russell that Zak was keeping bad company. When I relayed the news to Brandon, he turned it all on me, said I was to blame for being a lousy father, and why the hell didn't I disappear from their lives?"

"So then the fight?" I guessed. "Did Nathan Thorne's name come up?"

"Top of the list," Michael confirmed. "At that point Brandon totally lost control."

"And what about Zak's mom? Does she know that her youngest son is hanging out with Thorne?"

Massaging his temples and hiding his eyes from view, he shrugged. "I can't be sure. But there's something else—another reason for Brandon to lose control."

"Which is?"

"Sharon chose last night to yell at Zak big-time—about his suspension from school, his lack of respect, all the usual stuff. According to Brandon, Zak couldn't take it. He yelled back, threw stuff around the room, then ran out of the house."

"Ran where?" I asked.

"Nobody knows. He just ran. And he hasn't shown up since."

❧

Good, Darina. I'm glad you're focusing on this.

It was Phoenix again, hovering over my left shoulder as I drove. This time though, I had Michael in the car with me, so I couldn't enter into a full dialogue.

Find Zak, he went on. *Persuade him to go home, talk things through with Mom.*

"I have a hunch," I'd told Michael back in his crappy apartment. "I think I know where Zak might be." And I'd described the empty trailer in the park out on the road to Forest Lake.

Michael had sprung into action, ignoring the elevator and running downstairs two at a time, telling me to drive him straight there.

"I hope I'm right," I said now, to both Michael and Phoenix.

Trust your instinct, Phoenix murmured.

"Is there anything else I need to know?" Michael asked, leaning forward in his seat, one arm braced against the control panel.

"It's possible Zak's not alone. He might be there with Miller and Stafford, maybe even Nathan Thorne," I warned.

"They all know about this place. I get the idea it's where they regularly hang out."

"I'll deal with that," Michael promised. He was a father on a mission to redeem himself for ten years of absence.

He's like you, Phoenix, I thought. *He acts on impulse. He's a passionate guy.*

He's nothing like me, Phoenix protested.

"Drive faster," Michael pleaded as we passed the KFC and read the sign that said FOREST LAKE, 8 MILES.

Yeah, he is, I thought.

And I remembered the times I'd been driving with Phoenix in my old car, me observing the speed limit and him saying, "Drive, Darina. Let's see how fast this heap of rust can go!"

See! I told my Beautiful Dead boyfriend.

"We're almost there," I promised Michael as I turned off the highway onto a side road that narrowed and wound through pine trees. "You see the water up ahead? That's Forest Lake. The park is coming right up."

The words were hardly out of my mouth when we spotted the first trailer, set thirty feet back from the road in among the trees. There it was, complete with fancy mailbox and neatly fenced yard. I kept my foot on the gas, past more trailer homes, then one or two wooden shacks, and pretty soon we came to the deserted trailer where the kids hung out.

"Is this it?" Michael asked as I slowed down.

I nodded, took in the fact that there was no black Chevy parked outside, nor any other vehicle as far as I could see. Relieved, I decided to sit in the car and wait as Michael leaped out and ran toward the door.

I watched him knock first then try the handle. Nothing happened so he hammered on the door with his fist and finally bent down to pick up a rock lying at the foot of the metal steps. He used the rock to smash the glass panel in the door then he reached in and turned the handle from the inside.

It was at that exact moment that Zak charged the door.

He must have heard the knocking and stayed silent inside the trailer, waiting until the glass broke and Michael's hand had reached through. Then he knew it was time to act. So he ran at the door and sent his dad sprawling backward down the steps.

I saw it from a distance—Michael laid flat in the dirt and Zak stumbling, tripping over his father, sliding down the hill toward me. I got out of the car and was there to catch him when he finally came to a stop.

Angrily, Zak tried to wrench himself free.

I hung on to the hem of his sweatshirt, felt him twist, raise his arms, and slip out of it, saw him start running again until this time Michael cut him off. He tackled his son around the waist and brought him crashing down.

There we were, the three of us—me holding an empty sweatshirt, Michael grasping Zak in a bear hug, Zak lying motionless beneath him.

"No more running." Michael broke the silence. Slowly he relaxed his grip and knelt back to let his son recover.

I heard a breeze drift between the pines, saw the branches sway. *Good job, Darina!* Phoenix breathed.

"It's OK, Zak," I said. "Stick around and listen to what your dad has to say."

Breathing heavily, Zak rolled free of Michael and stood up. He was shorter than his dad, much skinnier. "What are you doing here?" he turned to me and demanded. "Who asked you to stick your nose in—again?"

"Don't talk to Darina that way," Michael cut in.

"And you don't get to tell me what to do!" Zak rounded on his dad. "Nobody does, not anymore."

"So that's it?" Warily Michael stood back. "You cut your family out of your life?"

"Since when were you my family?" Zak jeered. Now it didn't look like he would run, but neither was he ready to listen to what Michael had to say. "Do you even know what the word means?"

"OK, I hear you. And I don't blame you for being angry with me, Zak. But it's your mom I'm talking about. She deserves better."

"Oh yeah—Supermom."

"Zak! Your mother is there for you, always was."

"Not like you, huh?"

"Not like me," Michael agreed, forcing himself to meet Zak's stare. "What do you want—excuses? Because I don't have any."

"And now I should suck it up? Hey, no problem, Dad. Glad you're back. Why don't you stick around a little longer? We could share some quality time!"

Michael's head jerked back like a boxer dodging punches. Then he steeled himself for more.

Zak delivered. "Well, guess what? I did OK without you in the picture all these years."

"OK enough to end up here?" his dad muttered, glancing back at the trailer. "Take a look at yourself, Zak. This is not good."

"What do you know? What do you care?"

"I care. I always cared."

"Yeah, words. What do they mean exactly?"

Michael pursed his mouth up tight and frowned. When he spoke again, the phrases came out in painful jerks. "It means not a day goes by when I don't think about what I threw away when I walked out on your mom. Maybe not even an hour. For ten whole years I was this guy living alone thousands of miles away from the people he loved— floating, drifting, trying to find a reason to go on putting one foot in front of another. Not finding it."

Zak had turned his head away, but now he was definitely listening.

"You know how many times I moved on, working in one lousy job then another? After twenty new towns in Germany and Switzerland, France, Spain, I stopped counting."

"So? You're still the one who walked out. That doesn't change."

Michael nodded. "I'm not asking you to forgive me. I'm saying I still care. No, that's not the word."

Say it, I thought. *Tell him the right word.* I knew how I'd be feeling if it was my dad standing here trying to explain why he left. I would need to hear that word.

Michael dug deep. His voice wasn't much more than a whisper. "I *love* you, Zak. I love you, Brandon, and Phoenix more than my own life."

❧

Michael's apartment at Center Point wasn't much of a step

up from the empty trailer on the Forest Lake road, but no way was Zak ready to go back to his mom's house.

"I'm through with being treated like a little kid," he told his dad and me as I drove them back to town. "Being there—in that house—it messes with my head."

"So you can stay with me," Michael agreed. "I don't care, Zak, so long as you stay away from Nathan Thorne."

"I told your dad all about him," I confessed. "And his big brother, Oscar—he's the one to watch." Arriving at Michael's block, I parked and let them out of the car. I watched them enter the building with a feeling of relief.

Am I doing OK? I asked.

Silence. Phoenix didn't answer me.

From which I assumed that Hunter had called him back to Foxton again. *Hunter!* Suddenly my mind tuned into my daily mantra—*Hunter can't stop me now!*

Right now, in the current silence of the parking lot, I wasn't so sure. I stared at the row of overfilled trash cans, the graffiti walls, realizing I was a world away from the magic of Foxton, which is when the real panic set in.

"Hunter, don't listen to Phoenix," I said out loud. "I can deal with this."

Still silence.

"If you're thinking of giving up and pulling out of Foxton altogether, don't do it!" I begged. "I'm telling you—things are coming together. I've got a list of names I need to check out. There are people I have to see."

I was staring at the same old white plastic bag as before, eddying around the yard, whirling against my tires, flapping and drifting. And then I remembered, tomorrow was a big day for Hunter—the anniversary of his death.

I know what to do! I thought, turning the car and heading for home, straight to my laptop.

It didn't take me long to find a genealogy website called who-r-u.com, pay the subscription, and type in the name, Hester Lee, with an approximate birth date of 1905, place of birth, Foxton, mother's name, Marie, father's name, Hunter. Once and for all, with the recorded registration of Hester's birth I would settle Hunter's doubts and set his mind at rest.

Millions of people check their family history online, so the site was easy to use. I quickly followed the trail, found that Hester Lee married John Turner on June 28, 1925. The marriage certificate was signed on the bride's side by her aunt, Alice Harper. Her mother was listed as Marie Lee (deceased), her father as Hunter Lee, rancher, also deceased.

This should have been enough. It was official and beyond doubt—Hester was Hunter's daughter. And it made me wonder, had the overlord done this already? Surely, with his superpowers, he would have been able to check the certificate himself.

But then I thought, why not find out more? Staring at the names on the screen, it was an itch that had to be scratched. I tapped more keys and found that Hester and John had a daughter, Alice Marie, born January 5, 1927. Alice Marie Turner, an only child, married Wesley Ashton in August 1949. They had two children—Tom, born June 15, 1950, and Jane, born March 2, 1952. Jane Ashton, age eighteen and unmarried, gave birth in September 1970 to a baby girl named Laura. Jane died in childbirth.

I sat for an age, staring at the screen.

I wasn't focusing on a poor, lonely, cast-out kid named Jane who died giving life. No—Ashton is my mother's birth family name. Work it out carefully with me, go back through the generations. I am Marie and Hunter Lee's great-great-great granddaughter.

I sat at my computer and let day turn to night. I don't know how many times I checked the information and still came out with the same result.

How could I not? I always knew my mother's mother died giving birth to her. She was reared by her adoptive parents, Tom and Lucille Bunton. No one talked to her about her teenaged mother's pregnancy and death.

Obviously the Buntons found it too hard to discuss. And

Laura herself had conspired in this, carrying the burden of their secrecy all her life. As far as I knew, she never tried to discover more about her background than Tom and Lucille had been willing to tell.

I am descended from Marie and Hunter Lee. His blood runs in my veins.

❦

I set off before dawn on Tuesday to tell him.

He already knows! I told myself. *The way he looks at you. The photo of Marie. The fact that he ever let you through the barrier to meet the Beautiful Dead in the first place. Now it all comes together.*

Still I had no choice—I had to talk to Hunter.

My driving was crazy, my head in a spin. *I'm related to a walking dead man!*

The mountains loomed ahead. The road snaked around Turkey Shoot Ridge. A fire-red sun crept over the horizon.

At Foxton I turned left onto the dirt road, toward a bank of black cloud. It sat to the west over Amos Peak, threatening a big storm. Thirty feet below me, green water raced along the bed of the creek, swirling past boulders and kicking up white foam.

By the time I reached the aspen ridge, the first fat drops of rain hit my windshield. I abandoned my car under the trees and ran toward the water tower, fighting a strong wind, pushing on with my news, pulled along by the fierce new bond I'd forged with Phoenix's overlord.

I didn't for a second stop to wonder what Hunter's reaction would be.

The rain came fast now, battering the metal water tank, bouncing off the rocks. I staggered on, soaked to the skin and half blind, toward the house and barn, stepping back in my mind through decades to the day more than a hundred years earlier that Peter Mentone pulled a gun on Hunter and shot him through the head.

I ran through the meadow and across the yard. Rainwater cascaded from the roof of the barn; the cold wind drove into my face. Any moment now, Phoenix would step across my path, take my hand, and lead me to Hunter.

Or Iceman or Dean—one of the Beautiful Dead must surely appear. Yes, there was rain lashing across the valley and wind howling through the trees, but there was as of yet no thunder, no lightning. They were here on the far side, quietly sitting out the storm.

Was it raining like this all those years ago when Mentone arrived on horseback and found Marie alone in the house? Did he check the barn first, as I did now, to find out if Hunter was there?

I pictured the killer tethering his horse to the post and stepping through the wide door into a space stacked high in those days with hay and straw. The split log barn was new then, the smell of sawn pine filled the air. Hunter's ax, spades, forks, and scythe were stacked neatly against the wall. His horses' harnesses gleamed on their hooks.

Marie's horse grazed out in the meadow, but of Hunter's there was no sign.

Mentone knew he was in luck. He wasn't welcome here when his hardworking neighbor was home. With Marie, it was different—she usually had a smile on her lips and a few kind words for him. He heard the rain on the barn roof, dodged the waterfall spilling over the edge of the roof as he stepped back out across the yard.

Would he knock at the house door, as I did now, or would he turn the handle and walk right in? Marie would be standing at the stove with her back turned, or maybe upstairs working in the small bedroom. But then again— no. Even in the rain, with the door closed, she would have heard Mentone's horse approach. She would be facing him with a smile when he opened the door, ready to be polite.

"Peter, come in out of the wet. How are you doing today?"

"I'm good, Mrs. Lee. How about you?"

"Good too. Hunter isn't home, but I've got coffee on the stove if you'd like some."

He closes the door behind him. Somehow the rain

cuts them off and narrows the whole wide world to one small room with a rug on the floor, a lit stove, and a coffeepot boiling.

Mentone sees only Marie's face—her dark brown eyes fringed with thick lashes, her wide, smiling mouth. "Is there something I can do for you?" she offers.

He takes the coffee. In that split second, as her fingertips accidentally brush his, something clicks in his brain, and he decides to act on what he's been fantasizing about doing for a long, long time, which is to find Marie alone in the house and take much more than coffee. He drops the cup and grabs her around the waist. The cup smashes on the floor. Hot liquid spills.

Marie gasps and pulls back.

His arm is tight around her waist, her struggling excites him. He likes it when her coiled braid of almost black hair gets caught in the hook they use to hang the lantern from, her comb comes loose, and her hair tumbles down her back. He presses her against the window, she clutches at the curtain, brings the pole tumbling down.

There are no words from Marie after "Is there something I can do for you?" She's fighting to save herself, knowing why Mentone's here, realizing too late that he's been waiting for this moment—her alone, Hunter out since daybreak, and God alone knows when he'll be back. Marie kicks and scratches, but she doesn't scream. She's not made that way.

Mentone is stronger. He lets her fight a little—he's enjoying the fear in her eyes, her hair around her shoulders, the knowledge that he can raise her clean off her feet and do whatever he wants when he wants. He lifts her blue skirt, her white petticoats.

Hunter appears on the ridge. From under the aspens he sees Mentone's horse standing in the sheeting rain, gallops down the hill. He runs into the house, finds the two of them, Marie down on the floor and helpless, looking up at him like a hurt, trapped animal. Hunter rushes at Mentone, knocks him sideways, grapples with him, and pins him to the floor, kneels over him, raises his fists, and begins to punch him in the face and chest.

Marie is free. She gets to her feet and, afraid now that her husband will kill her attacker, tries to pull Hunter away, maybe even gives Mentone the split-second chance to free one arm, reach for his gun, aim, and fire.

Bang! *One shot. Hunter falls.*

Bang! *I hear it echo through the century. I see Hunter topple, hear Marie scream at last.*

Bang! It's not then but now. Not a shot from a gun, but the barn door slamming shut. I hear footsteps splashing through puddles.

The door to the house flies open and there stands Henry Jardine, with Sheriff Kors right behind him on the porch, and the rain hammering down.

7

After all the warnings I gave you?" Jardine quizzed. He stepped inside the house, glanced around at the table, the racks of dusty plates on the dresser, the unlit stove.

I came up with the usual lame excuse. "You know I don't sleep much. I'm following up my research."

Kors followed Jardine over the threshold, took off his hat, and shook the drips from the brim. "I take it you saw the two guys following you?"

I drew a sharp breath, shook my head, then tried to cover up the fear.

"A couple of guys on Harleys," Jardine went on. "We checked them out—the bikes are registered with Robert Black and Vincent Hall."

"Yeah? That's news to me." My comment was about as unconvincing as it's possible to be.

"They're on our radar." The sheriff walked to the bottom of the stairs. "We like to monitor their activities."

"So where are they now?"

"You lost them along the dirt road out of Foxton. We

watched them pull up by the creek then we drove on here ahead of them." Deciding not to check the upstairs room, Kors ran a finger along the dust on the table. "Don't you want to know the reason why we have Hall and Black in our sights? I'll tell you anyway. The day Phoenix Rohr was stabbed—they were present at the crime scene."

I made out I didn't know. "With a hundred other guys," I muttered. "Anyone in Ellerton under the age of twenty-five was there that day."

Kors gave me a hard look. "You act like you don't want us to find your boyfriend's killer."

The use of the *killer* word and the pressure of the situation suddenly got to me, and my legs buckled. Jardine slid a chair under me just in time to stop me from slumping to the floor. "Take it easy," he warned his boss, then turned back to me. "We're on your side, remember, Darina. All we want right now is for you to tell us why Oscar Thorne's guys are on your tail."

Drawing a deep breath, I started to explain. "It's complicated. You all know Oscar supplies…substances, illegal drugs to dealers in town. He spent time in jail for it last year. It didn't stop him from dealing. Now his kid brother, Nathan, acts as his go-between."

Jardine and Kors tucked away this useful piece of information. "And?" Kors asked.

"And Phoenix's brother, Zak, and a couple of other kids hang out with Nathan in an old trailer on the Forest Lake road. I happened to be there when Nathan pulled out a bag of white powder. I guess the situation quickly got back to Oscar, and he put Hall and Black onto me."

"These are people you do not—I repeat *not*—want to mix with." Jardine did his protective uncle thing, while Kors busily computed the facts. "Those two guys are suspected of being into everything you ever had nightmares about—drugs, automobile theft, serious assault, dangerous driving. So don't think that tailing you at a safe distance is all they have in mind."

It was my turn to process new information. "Why? What will they do to me?"

"How good is your imagination?" Kors interrupted. "Try staging a traffic accident for starters. A mysterious case of hit and run."

"Oh, God!" My legs trembled even more.

"Or mugging in broad daylight. And these guys carry serious weapons."

Up on the ridge, the first flash of lightning darted across the sky, followed by a growl of thunder. Rain drove onto the porch; wind rattled the windowpanes. Now I knew there was no chance of the Beautiful Dead sticking around on the far side.

For a while the sound of thunder drowned out the roar of

bike engines, and the first we saw of the Harley riders was through the frame of the open door when they were already halfway down the hill, about to cut across the meadow toward the house.

"Lucky for you we're here," Kors muttered, stepping out onto the porch.

The two bikers spotted him and his uniform. They reacted fast, wheeling away, back up the hillside, bouncing over the rough ground, swerving and leaning their bikes at crazy angles to negotiate the rocks and gullies.

Kors and Jardine ran up the hill after them. Their aim was to reach the car they'd parked out of sight under the aspens and chase Hall and Black out to Angel Rock.

Meanwhile, I stayed on the porch, shaking from head to foot. And this is how Hunter and Phoenix found me, soaking wet and terrified, when they braved the storm to come back to the far side.

❦

"I was right all along." Phoenix spoke to Hunter as they appeared in their halos of white light. "I told you this was too dangerous. Darina has to stop right now, before something really bad happens."

"Something bad has already happened," Hunter said. "She grew careless again. If this carries on, and outsiders keep coming here, our secret won't be secret anymore."

As the light around them faded, lightning flashed a second time. It forked through the black clouds, followed almost instantly by a sharp crack of thunder. "You shouldn't be here!" I cried.

"True," Hunter agreed, calm in spite of the danger he and Phoenix were in. "We only came to take care of the intruders you brought with you."

"Go back!" Guilt struck hard, and I ran to take both of Phoenix's hands to plead with him. Was it my imagination that he was paler, colder than ever, his grasp less strong?

"The storm is bad, and it's getting worse!"

"I can't leave until after I deal with our visitors," he whispered.

"So go up to the ridge," Hunter ordered. "Set up the barrier, drive all four of them away."

Phoenix had no choice—he must obey his overlord. "Wait here with Hunter," he told me, holding me by the shoulders and forcing me to look straight into his eyes.

"The guys on the bikes didn't get past Angel Rock before they wrecked their machines. The cops didn't even make it that far."

I hung on to his hands, desperate not to let him go.

"You're sure? You can hear what's happening?"

He nodded then pulled free. "Wait here," he said again then strode out.

I ran to the door after him, watched him sprint across the drenched meadow and up the hill as another fork of lightning flickered across the sky.

"This isn't right!" I went to plead with Hunter, who stood impassively by the window. His face was blank, and his eyes stone cold. "The electric storm—Phoenix won't make it through!"

"He knows what he has to do," Hunter muttered. "If he fails, you understand what will happen."

The storm will overpower him. The electrical charge of the lightning will drain his superhuman strength. Death will claim him.

"So was it worth it?" Hunter asked me calmly as he read my thoughts. "Really, Darina—whatever you came here to tell me, was it worth risking everything for?"

"Judge for yourself." I gathered every shred of willpower to stand up to his challenge. "My main reason for coming was you, Hunter. I found out everything you need to know about Hester—I checked the details on her birth certificate. You're named as her father."

You know what happens when you strike a strong man hard? His eyelids flicker, but he hardly flinches. That was how it was when I gave Hunter this news.

"How much more certain can you be that she was your daughter and not Mentone's?" I asked.

"I hear you."

"And did you ever check the certificate for yourself? You could have found a way to do that."

He shook his head.

"Why not?"

"Because."

I stared at Hunter, suddenly seeing him in a different light and connecting his hesitancy with Phoenix's seeming reluctance to pursue his own killer. "Were you scared of what you might find?" I stammered. "If it turned out that Mentone was Hester's father, would you really have wanted to know?"

"The facts aren't always easy to handle," he admitted.

"But this certificate makes it official," I insisted. "Marie wouldn't lie to the registrar, right?"

Hunter shook his head. "My wife never told a lie in her entire life."

"So she was one hundred percent certain that you were the father. And maybe Mentone's attack didn't go as far as actual rape."

I waited a while for him to work through the implications of what I'd said.

"Aren't you glad?" I asked.

He breathed deep. "It's good to learn the truth. Thank you."

Two precious words of gratitude fell from Hunter's lips! *Yes, it was worth it*, I thought, spurred on to say more. "Hester married in 1925. She had a daughter named Alice Marie."

Silently Hunter mapped the life he would have had as a father and grandfather, but he gave no sign of how it made him feel. Instead, he gazed at me with expressionless features, as if listening to someone else's history, far removed from his own.

"Alice Marie married Tom Ashton." My stomach tightened as I reached the end of the story. "They had one son and one daughter, Tom and Jane."

He gave the slightest nod, his gray eyes penetrating deep into my psyche. Knowing full well what was in my head, he did at least let me say it out loud.

"Jane Ashton was my grandmother. We belong to the same family, you and I." I spoke the words and waited for Hunter's reaction, longing for him to reach out and take my hand. Instead, he simply went on staring deep into my eyes.

"You want to know my reaction?" he asked at last, speaking quietly then turning to watch the latest lightning hit over Amos Peak. "This is hard for you, Darina, but I have to remind you of something that I told you the first time we spoke, almost a year ago. You talked then of loving Phoenix and of him loving you from beyond the grave."

"You didn't believe me," I recalled. "You said that for love to exist there has to be a heart."

"And the Beautiful Dead have no beating heart, no blood running through their veins. What I'm saying is—we have no emotions. It's impossible for us to be glad or sad, for me to tell you truthfully that I'm happy about the family link between us."

"That's true for you, maybe," I argued, fighting back the hurt his words had caused. "But not for Phoenix and the rest. They have feelings even after they die. Remember Jonas—how much he still cared for Zoey? And Arizona— she came across as hard and cynical, but even she wouldn't rest until she knew her kid brother was safe. Also Summer— she needed her parents to look to the future, to go on and live their lives without her."

As for my beautiful Phoenix, he tells me he will stay with me. He will be in the air I breathe, will walk beside me always.

"So I'm wrong?" Hunter asked, as if this was the first time he'd allowed the possibility to enter his head and the idea amused him.

"Totally. The Beautiful Dead do have feelings. Why else would they want to return to the far side?" I waited a while, carefully watching Hunter's face, wanting those hard, chiseled lines to soften. "It's been a long time since you died. And you're the overlord. To you, sharing your feelings might seem like weakness."

The shadow of a smile appeared. "You sure know how to frame an argument," he said. "Just like my Marie."

Slowly I regained my courage and smiled back. "You always knew we were linked. No way is this news to you."

"I suspected. I *hoped*."

Hoped? I felt my heart swell. Hunter wanted me to be family. In spite of what he said, he cherished the bond between us.

"Yes, hoped." For a second his features did change. There was a moment's tenderness in the overlord's steely eyes. Then lightning flashed, thunder crashed, and he was all hardness again. He listened. Through the crash of thunder he must have heard what was happening at Angel Rock. "Phoenix needs help," he said abruptly, striding toward the door.

I ran after him, my heart shuddering. "What's happening? Is he OK?" I asked.

"Come with me," Hunter instructed, and we went out into the downpour, heading up to the ridge as fast as we could.

I struggled to keep up, slipping and sliding on the wet rocks, but Hunter reached the aspen stand way before me and disappeared over the ridge.

"Wait for me!" I begged.

He strode on toward Angel Rock—that dark granite outcrop in the shape of a Christmas-tree angel, silhouetted against the bank of thunderclouds, lit by sudden flashes of lightning.

"Phoenix, please be OK!" I whispered, following in

Hunter's footsteps until I caught sight of him again. In the distance, north of Angel Rock, I glimpsed two abandoned Harleys and some dark figures fighting.

Another bolt of lightning struck and thunder rattled. I grew more frightened still as I rushed after Hunter—how long could he and Phoenix go on in the eye of the storm? I fought my exhaustion, forced myself onward until at last I reached Angel Rock.

The first figure I identified through the sheet of rain was Henry Jardine. He emerged from behind the tall rock, staggering backward with his arms raised to protect his head. Phoenix followed him, towering over him and concentrating his zombie powers on beating Jardine back down the hillside with invisible wings and a horde of death-heads.

I heard Jardine cry out—a mixture of pain and terror—then fall backward onto a flat slab of glistening wet granite where he curled into a ball, rolled, and lay helpless.

Phoenix followed, stood astride the deputy sheriff, glared down on him, and zapped him with the mind-bending rays that would rob him of all memory of this event. I held my breath as the supernatural charge hit Jardine and passed through him, making him jolt and writhe. Then Phoenix bent forward to grasp his arm and raise him from the ground, lifting him with ease.

There was no struggle left in the deputy sheriff—in a daze

he allowed himself to be turned away from Angel Rock and led along the ridge by Phoenix, who eventually released him under the aspens and watched him walk unsteadily toward his car.

Meanwhile, I saw Hunter deal with Hall and Black. On foot, away from their Harleys and battered by the storm, the two tough guys didn't look so dangerous. They ran across the scrub in my direction, stumbling as I had, yelling and acting like they'd seen a ghost. Close behind them came Hunter, seemingly strong as ever, gaining on his victims with every stride. When he drew near enough, he brought the death-heads hurtling down out of the dark sky—ghastly yellow skulls crowding in on Black and Hall, forcing them onto their knees, making them crouch and beg for mercy.

They were wasting their breath. Hunter seized them, one in either hand, and dragged them back on their feet. He flung them against Angel Rock, knocking the last remaining air out of their lungs, pinning them there as he zapped their brains, making them curl up and scream.

"Phoenix, take Darina down to the house," Hunter ordered without looking around. "And when you're sure she's safe, leave the far side."

"What about you?" Phoenix asked.

"I can deal with this. Just go!"

So Phoenix turned and ran with me, down from Angel

Rock into the valley where the invisible wings didn't beat and the death-heads melted away into the dark sky. We reached the meadow, and I clung to him, sobbing with relief.

"Don't cry," he murmured, brushing strands of wet hair from my cheek. He put his arms around me and held me until I stopped.

"We're almost there," I gasped, pointing toward the house. "Leave me. Do what Hunter told you."

"First I take you inside," he insisted.

We reached the yard with the rain still beating down and thunder rumbling down from the mountains.

"Really, it's time to go," I begged. "Phoenix, please!" He seemed to falter then recover as he kept hold of my hand and walked on. "Hunter said to take you to the house."

"But you're losing strength. You need all your energy to get out of here." To step away from the far side, back into limbo, where he would be safe until the storm was over.

We were on the porch. I was struggling to free my hand from his—Phoenix swayed, put out his other hand to steady himself against the porch rail. Pain flashed across his beautiful features, creasing his brow.

"Go now!" I cried.

"I can't bear to leave you." He sighed, stepping back to let his head rest against the log wall of the cabin, letting the raindrops trickle down his face. "I want to stay here with you."

I shook my head. "You can't. Hunter said to go."

"I want to be with you," he insisted, letting his eyes close and drawing an uneven breath. "I'm clinging to every moment we have together, Darina. Don't turn me away."

I went to him, put my arms around his neck, and tried to make him listen. "I'll be here when the storm ends. We can be together then."

Phoenix put his cheek cold against mine. "It's too hard." He groaned. "When I'm with you, it's ecstasy. When we're apart, I'm in agony. And all the time I'm afraid."

"Afraid of what?" I whispered. Outside the storm raged, but here under the porch, I felt safer.

"Of what happens next. I have three days left on the far side—that's all."

"I know. But, like I told Hunter, I'm making new contacts, finding out facts, pushing for answers…"

He stopped me by gently brushing his fingers over my lips. "That's not what I mean. I'm not scared that you won't solve the mystery because I know in my heart that you will work at it until you do. No, the bottom line is, I'm not certain anymore that I even want to find out who killed me because the price may be too high for my mom, for Zak, for Brandon."

Startled, I took a step back. "It's what I told Hunter— you can't be scared of the truth. I thought we all agreed— we need to know!"

But he shook his head. "It's weird—lately it's begun to feel kind of irrelevant and unreal. And I'll tell you what else really scares me, Darina—what happens next? It's the big question, what comes afterward—after my twelve months are finally up?"

After you step away from the far side for the last time, after you return to limbo—what then? "No one knows, do they?" I whispered back. "Not even Hunter."

"Being like this—being Beautiful Dead, isn't how you imagine," Phoenix murmured. "Superstrength, super-hearing, time travel—in the beginning it blows your mind. You think you're invincible."

"Then it ends."

"And you realize you're not all-powerful. You're just like any other human being, only you get to die twice."

I stepped in and clung to him again. "I understand," I murmured. "It's good that you're telling me. You know what I think? It's normal to be scared. I'm certain that's how Jonas felt, and Arizona and Summer. But what will keep you strong, what will get you through is this feeling we have between us—you and me."

His hands cupped my head, and he gazed at me in silence.

"That's what you always tell me," I told him. "You say that what survives, long after we're gone, is love."

We held each other until the overlord strode down from the ridge with Danny Kors behind him.

I saw them and tore myself away from Phoenix. "What's wrong with Hunter?" I cried, running back into the rain.

He was striding across the meadow, one arm hanging limp at his side. His face was white, his eyes dark and hollow.

He didn't speak. Brushing past me as more lightning forked across the sky, he stepped onto the porch, and with what was obviously a fast-reducing reserve of strength, he ordered Phoenix to leave. "Do it," he hissed. "Get out of here before it's too late!"

Phoenix shook his head and took a step in my direction. Then Hunter blasted him with angry force, sent him reeling sideways along the porch, surrounded him in their shimmering energy field, and made him fade and disappear.

The look of mingled hope and sadness that Phoenix gave me as he lay on the porch surrounded by white light broke my heart in two.

And now Phoenix was gone and Kors had crossed the meadow. He spotted me with Hunter and drew his gun. "Darina, get away from there. Stand clear!"

I froze on the step of the porch. "You don't understand. Don't do this! Don't shoot!"

"It's OK," Hunter said quietly as he stepped in front of me. Now that Phoenix was safe from the storm, he could give the sheriff his full focus. So he leveled his gaze on the gun barrel and walked slowly toward him.

Kors's right hand held steady as Hunter advanced. His arm was braced, his left hand lending support. "One more step and I shoot."

The overlord walked on. His only intention was to send Kors out of here a second time with a sore head and blank memory. One step, two steps, three…

The sheriff fired his gun, his hand jerked from the recoil.

The bullet hit Hunter in the shoulder and passed clean through—no wound, no blood. He carried on walking. Four steps, five…

Kors fired again. He hit his second target—the center of Hunter's chest. Again the bullet passed through without a mark.

Hunter didn't flinch. He advanced with steel-cold, unblinking eyes, reached out, and took the gun from Kors as if he was taking a toy from a child. Then he threw it to one side and swept the sheriff off his feet, sending him crashing against the side of the rusted truck parked at the side of the house. I heard the impact, saw him slump to the ground.

Then I witnessed something I'd never seen before. Hunter stood astride Kors, one arm still limp and with a look of exhaustion on his face. The storm had seriously weakened him, I realized, and he'd reached the limits of his strength.

163

Still he had to wipe his victim's memory and escort him out of here. But the overlord's shoulders sagged, and it looked like he didn't have the energy.

Was this it? Was Hunter going to fail? I took a step toward him and felt him raise invisible wings to beat me back.

Fading then fighting back, summoning his strength, he gazed down at Kors and surrounded him with dazzling white light. The sheriff groaned and tried to raise himself. Hunter intensified the light. Kors slumped back, sighed, and vanished.

The wings beat all around me. The storm raged. Hunter tilted back his head and let the rain stream down his face.

"Go quickly!" I gasped, unable to move from the shelter of the porch.

He turned his head toward me. His eyes were dull and blank—they told me that it was already too late. Wings surged over me. Hunter stood under the storm, gazing up at the dark heavens.

Lightning darted down. It struck the water tower on the ridge with a terrifying flash. The air crackled. Hunter swayed but didn't move from the spot.

Go! I prayed.

He stood like a tree in a storm—swaying, bending in the wind and rain. He seemed to be waiting.

Thunder filled the valley, crashed around us, and rolled

on. Then lightning split the sky, once, twice in quick succession, and the deafening clap came with it—two flashes of blinding light, a giant's roar. Hunter stood alone at the edge of the meadow, staring at the sky, illuminated then plunged back into darkness, lit up again by nature's fury.

Fight! I pleaded. *Don't let this happen to you!*

He turned his head again and looked at me, growing too weak even to keep up the barrier of wings that held me on the porch. The beating wings faded, releasing me so that I could run out into the rain to be at his side.

When I reached him, he didn't meet my gaze but turned his head away.

"Look at me!" I pleaded.

The storm was wild around us, rain lashed us, stung our faces, and drenched us through.

"I can't lose you—not now!" I whispered as I clung to Hunter's arm. "Don't you know how we look up to you—all of us?"

He answered in a voice already thousands of miles away, spinning with the planets in vast black space.

"Everything comes to an end."

"No. We're not finished. You have to take care of Phoenix."

"Others will come," he promised. As he turned again and looked at me, the faded death-wing tattoo on his temple seemed to darken, his skin to grow ghastly white.

"Phoenix needs *you!*" I told him.

"Don't talk now," he whispered, raising his hand to my cheek and looking deep into my eyes, swaying again and sighing with the wind.

His touch was icy cold. Dark blood began to trickle from the place on his temple where Mentone's bullet had entered.

The wind drove on and rolled the storm clouds out of the valley and up onto the next ridge. Above us the sky began to lighten.

"Listen to me, Darina," Hunter said, gazing steadily at me, the last glimmers of light fading from his eyes. "I chose you to help the Beautiful Dead, and it was a good choice. You didn't let us down. No one could have shown more courage, more devotion."

I felt anguished tears rise and let them fall down my cheeks. *Please stay!*

"If I've been harsh in the past, it was not to blame you, but for the good of the others," he explained. "For Jonas, Arizona, Summer, and Phoenix. My job above all else was to keep our secret and to protect them."

I understand. Above our heads, wisps of white cloud trailed after black.

Hunter gazed at me with deep tenderness. "I have always believed in you."

I saw the inner light fade to nothing, felt his strong hand tremble. Determined to stand until the end came, he braced himself against a sudden wind that gusted across the yard.

Stricken and helpless, I lost hope.

Hunter's eyelids flickered. A light seemed to surround him—that miraculous glimmer.

"It's time to say good-bye," a voice told me.

I glanced around and saw Dean stride out of the barn toward us.

Hunter's grip finally loosened. He was still gazing at me as his body melted in a halo of silver light.

8

There's no reason to be sad," Dean said. He stayed with me after Hunter departed, leading me into the barn, up the stairs into the loft where we quietly watched blue skies take the place of storm clouds over the aspen ridge.

"This is part of the unchanging cycle—Hunter's time is finished. I take his place. And you're right, Darina—it can never be the same."

"I didn't even think that," I protested.

"Not yet," Dean agreed. "But you will. What you feel for Hunter is unique. Keep it in your heart and cherish it."

I glanced at the new overlord. His voice seemed to have deepened, his face was sterner than before. His short hair was steel gray, his grayish-blue eyes shone from under a straight, strong brow. Like all the Beautiful Dead, his skin was white and smooth as ivory.

Dean held my gaze. "Do you want to continue?" he asked.

"What do you mean?"

"To go on with the task. I talked with Phoenix just now, and he expressed his doubts. So I need you to tell me honestly, Darina—do you still want to use the days we have left to release Phoenix from limbo and send him safely on?"

"Or…?"

"Or stop now. Go home and be safe."

"You already know the answer," I told him. "Phoenix means everything to me. I don't understand why you even have to ask."

"Because, whether you acknowledge it or not, there is a choice, and I need you to think about it." Dean spoke like the cop he used to be when he was alive—slow and measured, aiming to take the heat out of my angry reply.

"I do realize how much Phoenix means to you."

"I love him," I said fiercely.

"And there's the old saying about love being blind. All I'm pointing out is the other side of things, like the fact that this time around Phoenix isn't one hundred percent certain he wants to continue."

"Neither was Summer," I pointed out. "She thought maybe it was too painful for her mom. And Jonas—he thought he was hurting Zoey. This is nothing new."

"With Phoenix, the doubt is stronger," Dean argued. "Besides, this time you've placed yourself in real danger. Any more pressure from you, and who knows how guys like Oscar and Nathan will react."

"I've thought about it. I've talked it through with Phoenix. Why won't anybody listen to me?"

Dean fell silent for a while, pacing slowly between the window and the wooden stairs then back again. "Let me give you some background," he said quietly. "These are things I learned through my job, working alongside Henry Jardine in the Shepherd County sheriff's office. Number one, the drug scene in Ellerton is run by ruthless professionals. Behind Oscar Thorne there's a network of international suppliers who possess nothing you or I would recognize as a decent moral code—zero honesty, loyalty, or compassion. Around here Thorne might act like the big guy, but in the world of drug running he's expendable—one bullet to the head and *bang!*"

"So?" I demanded. "Why are you focusing on this? What does it have to do with who stabbed Phoenix?"

"A fight like that, flaring up between rival gangs at a gas station—it might seem spur of the moment, but often there's a long history, fed by greed and revenge. Say, for instance, Oscar's kid brother, Nathan, is already a known drug mule. The day Phoenix is killed, someone knows the kid's carrying stuff in his car. This someone—Phoenix maybe—grabs a split-second opportunity to snatch the package—let's say it's worth a cool five grand—from the glove compartment. One of Oscar's guys catches him in the act. Five thousand dollars is a lot of money—certainly enough to draw a knife for."

The pit of my stomach churned as I pictured the scene.

"Phoenix wouldn't do that. He wasn't into drugs."

"So someone else. Let's say it was a flashpoint."

"Do you know this for sure, or are you guessing?" I wanted to know.

"It was a definite line of inquiry when I was alive."

"But no one who was there at the scene will open up to the cops."

Dean nodded. "That's how it works. And I'm telling you this because part of me agrees with Phoenix—this scene is way too big and complicated for you to unravel. And even if you did, and you make Nathan Thorne a prime suspect, there are still guys like Vince Hall and Robert Black to bring into the equation."

Sighing wearily, I tried to prepare myself. "So tell me the bad news about those two."

"They're both heavy users of cocaine. Oscar supplies them, obviously."

"And…?"

"They're into Harleys, as you know. But Hall was once the owner of the black Chevrolet now driven by Nathan Thorne."

"I know the car you mean."

"Hall liked to get out of his head on crack cocaine then jump in the Chevy and drive up the jeep road to the summit of Amos Peak. He did it for kicks. It was just my luck that one day I was on duty out there when Vince chose to take Black with him on one of his joyrides. He saw my patrol car up ahead and was not happy about me stepping out to talk with him."

"You'd already radioed the registration number back to the office," I murmured, digging deep in my memory for something Jardine had once told me. "But somehow that information was lost from the record."

Dean nodded. "Vince was so unhappy to see me that he totally forgot to put his foot on the brake."

"He ran you down?"

"Without a second's hesitation," the new overlord agreed with a wry smile. "Stopping to talk would've spoiled their day, considering they had a quantity of illegal drugs on them at the time. Plus, they never would've got to the top of Amos Peak without a clear run at the summit."

***

"I carry on." This is what I would say to Phoenix when he returned after the storm. I wouldn't need to speak the words—he would look into my eyes and know.

I waited in the barn with Dean, watching the sky clear some more, remembering Hunter's last conversation with me before he left the far side for good. "Hunter believed in me," I murmured. "He told me that himself."

"Then you have a lot to live up to," Dean said quietly.

He stood in the doorway, watching the sun sink and turn the sky pinkish gold. Rainwater still dripped from the roof, and steam rose from the wet, warm earth.

Behind us, in the dark space of the old barn, gentle wings began to beat. I held my breath and waited.

"We return to the far side," Iceman and Phoenix chanted, emerging out of the magical light. "We are back from beyond the grave."

I gasped and ran to Phoenix, eager to have his arms around me.

"Hunter is safe," Iceman told Dean. "We watched him travel on. He was at peace."

"The world turns," Dean said. "Nothing stays the same."

"You understand what happened to him?" Phoenix murmured, holding me tight and gazing down at me.

"Kind of. He saved you, but the storm was too strong to save himself."

He held me close to his smooth, cold chest. "Not only that. Hunter learned the truth about Marie and his daughter so his time on the far side had run its course. Dean was ready to take his place."

Still it was hard to believe that I'd never again see Hunter's tall, strong figure stride along Foxton Ridge or set eyes on those features that seemed carved out of stone.

"I'll miss him more than I can say."

"I hear you."

Looking into Phoenix's clear eyes the color of the evening sky, I spoke out loud words he'd already read in my heart. "I'll never forget Hunter."

"Likewise," Phoenix whispered. "We—the Beautiful Dead—owe him everything."

❧

Thursday was almost here, and everyone was texting me.

COME TO MY PLACE, 2NITE 6:30—LUV ZOE

U OWE ME COFFEE—HANN

XOX MEET 4 CATCH UP—JORDAN

Surrounded by packing cases, watching Laura take down pictures from the walls, I texted them back to say I was busy moving.

GOD, DARINA, HOW COME? Hannah texted.

U CANNOT BE SERIOUS! Jordan said.

WHEN? WHERE 2? CALL ME! Zoey insisted.

I turned off my phone without replying.

"We have to be out of here Sunday," Laura told me early Wednesday morning, after I'd slept on my return from Foxton. She handed me a black garbage bag. "Go through your closet, throw out anything you don't need."

I went into my room, sat on the bed, and heard her scraping furniture across the floor and dumping stuff in boxes until Jim came back and took her off to sign papers in the realtor's office. Then I stared at the pots of makeup on my table and my necklaces hanging to one side of the mirror, and for some reason, the small white fear-stone with the hole in it—the one in Kim Reiss's dish of pebbles—came into my head and wouldn't go away.

"Hey, you're only moving!" I muttered. How could I be scared by putting things in boxes after all the Beautiful Dead drama I'd been through?

Exactly! Arizona-in-my-head said. *What's the big deal?*

Summer-in-my-head saw beneath the surface. *Moving is always stressful*, she said gently. *This is the last thing Darina needs right now.*

"Thanks," I told her. Then someone knocked at the door, and I went down to answer it.

"Can I come in?" Sharon Rohr asked.

I swear she didn't come to my house with the exact aim of yelling at me and telling me how much she hated me. She probably thought she could hold herself together and have a rational conversation expressing her point of view, but it turned out she couldn't.

She was hardly through the door before her voice cracked. "I'm here for one reason, and only one," she began.

I nodded, stepped back, and let her walk into the kitchen. "Zak's with his dad—you got the news?"

"I heard. Don't expect any thanks from me."

"I don't." Trying hard not to provoke her, I switched on the coffee machine. "At least it beats hanging out with Nathan Stone."

"Says who?" This was Sharon's first ever visit to my house, and she was looking around, taking in the packing boxes and bare walls. "Since when did my lousy ex suddenly gain the status of good influence?"

"I hear you, but if it's a choice between drug dealers and—"

"Darina, you don't get it." She stopped taking in her surroundings and came close. "What you have to understand is that what you think doesn't matter anymore. What I came here to say is—you're out of our lives, if you were ever in it."

"That's what you came here to tell me?" I got out coffee cups with trembling hands, swallowed hard. "I'm sorry. I was only trying—"

Sharon raised both hands as if pushing me away.

"Don't try. Don't speak. Listen to me. You are responsible for a lot of bad things in my life, and this latest is pretty hard to swallow. I never in a million years thought I would lose Zak to my ex-husband."

In the background the coffee machine swished and

gurgled. Sharon's words knocked me so far off balance I was speechless. I stared silently at her face—not pale and guarded as usual, but sparking anger. In fact, she seemed in all ways more energized, someone to take notice of at last, after a lifetime of being walked over.

"I mean, where was Michael all these years? How can Zak walk out on me to be with him?"

"You wish I'd never shown Michael where Zak was hanging out?" I whispered.

"Exactly!" she hissed. "Just like I wish you'd never gotten together with Phoenix in the first place."

"Stop," I pleaded. She'd crossed the line—no way was I staying silent after this. "I'm sorry you feel this way—I really am. But you have to stop blaming me."

"Why? You trapped him. After he went with you, he stopped making his own decisions. He didn't live his own life."

I shook my head and told it like it was. "I didn't hook Phoenix on a line—he was free, and he chose me. We were happy."

Sharon reacted like I'd hit her in the stomach, hunching her skinny shoulders and crossing her arms to protect herself.

"He chose me," I repeated. "And Zak didn't just go to stay with Michael because I persuaded him. He went because staying in your house was messing with his head."

She drew breath then sat down on the one chair that wasn't piled high with boxes. "How can you say that?"

"Those were his words, not mine. I don't think you know how tough this has been for Zak."

"I look out for him. I work hard at it."

"I'm not saying you don't. But I guess he's listened to one too many fights—between you and Michael before he left, then between you and Brandon, you and Phoenix, now you and him. That's it, he's through with arguing."

"So now I'm the bad guy?" She gasped.

"No. You were fighting to hold it together, raising three boys—I appreciate that. But maybe Zak doesn't see it that way, not right now. And he was hurting and hanging out with the wrong people."

What I was saying seemed to get through to Sharon.

"How come I couldn't find a way to stop it from happening? It's like they slid into that, one by one—first Brandon, then Phoenix, now Zak."

"All kids look for trouble," I argued. "A few get caught."

Sharon bit her lip and looked back over the recent family history. "They stuck a label on us right from the start. 'The Rohrs are back in town. Watch out, it means trouble.'"

"I think that's right. That's the way Phoenix saw it, too."

She sat up straight and looked at me like she was seeing me for the first time. "He talked to you about family problems?"

"Yeah, we covered just about everything, him and me."

That's love. That's finding your soul mate. "I was lucky."

"I never knew that." She sighed. "Sure, I could see why he was attracted to you—you're a beautiful girl. But I thought it was skin-deep."

"You didn't think it would last?" I smiled sadly. *It's lasted way beyond the grave, let me tell you.*

"He was so young. You were his first real girl."

"So you have to forgive me," I told her with a shrug.

"For what?"

"For coming into Phoenix's life."

Closing her eyes, Sharon let out a short laugh, and in that moment, some of the bad feeling she had toward me seemed to melt away. "Yeah, I guess I do."

"And I'll tell you something else."

She opened her eyes and looked expectantly at me.

"If you want my opinion, Zak won't stay long in Michael's apartment. He'll come home to you—I bet you a million bucks."

Sometimes the voices in my head speak louder than real life. After Sharon left for Michael's apartment to enter into negotiations with her ex, I drove out of town to the eco-burial site where Byron Lavelle had laid Logan to rest.

Why here? Arizona-in-my-head asked as I parked my car among the tall redwoods and walked up the hill.

Back off, Arizona. Darina needs some time to think. This was Jonas talking from the place where the Beautiful Dead finally go. *She loves it here. It's so peaceful.*

It's true—I do. The tall trees rise straight and meet overhead like a cathedral roof. The granite rocks sparkle pink, silver, and white.

I feel close to Logan here.

"Who'd have thought it?" I murmured to him. "Sharon Rohr is speaking to me. At last I'm not the enemy."

Logan wasn't Beautiful Dead, but that didn't stop me from talking to him. When he was alive, he was the closest thing to a brother I'd ever known. He was the grounded, sensible one whose advice I resented, the kid I'd known since kindergarten.

"She's visiting Zak as we speak," I went on, gazing up at the swaying branches. "She and Michael will have to work together to help him through this period. Zak will have to face a few facts about the way he's been acting."

Crazy-girl Darina, Arizona laughed.

Go ahead—Logan hears you, Jonas urged.

"The rest is pretty scary," I admitted. "There's talk of civil war inside Oscar Thorne's drug gang, and no one will stand up and tell the truth. That's what's getting in my way right now."

Sitting cross-legged under the trees, I breathed in the

smell of pine needles and resin. I remembered Logan—the way he drove me mad by showing up on my porch with advice and support. And I saw his face and open smile under the mop of brown curly hair.

"What would you do?" I asked him. "Would you go after the two Harley guys, or would you put more pressure on others who were there—Zak, Brandon, Nathan, maybe even the girl behind the cash desk again? I have two days to do this, remember."

Logan would say, be safe. Look out for yourself. Arizona was right, of course. She was always the smartest person I knew.

"Being safe isn't an option," I argued. "That's what I told Dean and Phoenix. Doesn't it seem weird to you, how Phoenix doesn't get how I feel? This is the first time it's happened, and it's driving me crazy."

For once no one responded with an answer, and I had to find comfort in just staring up at the patterns the branches made against the blue sky. I wanted support, advice, and encouragement, but it was clear this time that I would have to decide for myself.

In the end I left Logan's burial site and decided to track down the youngest Rohr. Zak had the most reasons to agree to talk to me, if only I could get him to see it this way after Sharon had paid him the visit she'd been planning. What I didn't predict was that the thing had turned into a full-scale family conference, Brandon included.

I knocked on the door of apartment 209.

Brandon opened it. "You should get a job at the United Nations," he told me.

I had to think this one through before I understood what he was getting at. "Ha—funny! Is Zak here?"

"Bro, here comes the peace broker," he called over his shoulder, ready to step out of my way then suddenly changing his mind. "So it looks like you got free access to the Rohrs. I don't know what you did, but Mom has done a U-turn. She suddenly has you down as flavor of the month."

"Is she still here?" I asked. As usual, Brandon set my nerves on edge with his suspicious tone and the mocking curl of his lip.

"She already left."

"What did they decide?"

"Zak stays here until Sunday then they all talk again about him moving back to the house." He leaned against the doorframe, muscles looking pumped under his white T-shirt. "Congratulations, Darina. It looks like the kid is back walking the line."

"What about Michael? Is he home?"

Brandon shook his head. "He's playing golf. You know, I've been thinking maybe you were right about something—you don't need me to look after you anymore. It seems you're all grown up now."

"Why do I think that's not a compliment?" I asked warily. With Brandon there was always the chance of a below-the-belt blow to follow. "Does this mean you want the car back?"

"Oh, Darina, that's so not cool." He faked disappointment that I could be so petty. "The car comes with no strings. All I'm saying is that it's been a year now, like we said, and I can't be your babysitter forever."

"No matter what you promised Phoenix?" I said without meaning to. The sly words just slipped out.

If he was hurt, Brandon didn't show it. "Whoa, what happened to the diplomacy skills? Yeah, whatever I said to my brother, I figure I kept that promise, and it's time for you to take care of yourself."

"I totally agree," I muttered. *Don't do me any favors. Don't think that I need you in any way whatsoever!*

With a satisfied grin, Brandon launched himself free of the doorjamb and brushed past me. "Don't pressurize the kid," he warned with a nod over his shoulder toward the living room. "Zak is still on a short fuse, so don't push him—OK?"

I gritted my teeth and let Brandon go. He was halfway down the corridor, heading for the escalator when he remembered something else. "Russell Bishop was here," he said casually.

"To play golf with Michael?" Why should this mean anything to me?

"Yeah, Ralph Lauren–man. He had an interesting piece of news that he wanted to share."

"Which was?"

"Early this morning, the cops went to Nathan Thorne's house and arrested him for drugs. I thought you should know."

I went inside, and Zak made it plain that he wasn't excited to see me. He lay sprawled in the one brown chair in front of a small TV screen, hardly bothering to turn his head when I said hi.

"I heard the news about Nathan," I said to grab Zak's attention away from the cartoon channel. Actually, I was shocked that Sheriff Kors had acted, presumably, on the information I'd provided. *Come back, Brandon—I need you to look out for me after all!* was one of my first thoughts.

"You talked to the cops," Zak muttered, eyes still glued to the screen.

"Not me," I lied.

"Yeah, you did." The velour chair was on a swivel base, and he turned it to face me. "That's how come they arrested him."

"So what if I did? Everyone knows Nathan Thorne is heading the same way as his brother." Somehow saying this and bringing it out into the open eased the tension between us. "I'm glad you were only on the edge of that scene at the trailer. Plus, it was cool I knew where to find you a couple of days back. Maybe now things will work out for you."

Zak did the Rohr shrug and brought Phoenix's image flooding into my head.

Keep talking, Darina, Phoenix said, as if he was right there, backing every word. *Zak listens to you, even if he doesn't admit it.*

"Phoenix would be happy," I told Zak. "He would want you out of that trailer, back with your family."

Another shrug. "Mom and Dad are talking again," he said. "How about that?"

"I know. I'm shocked—in a good way."

"He says he can give her an allowance."

"Is that what she wants?"

"To send me to college when I reach eighteen. He had a security job in Berlin. That's how come he saved the dough."

"Cool. And is that what *you* want?"

"Engineering school would be good, I guess. Building roads and bridges. I need to go back to school first though. Mom's gonna talk to Valenti."

"All excellent," I said. "Zak—that's so cool."

"It didn't happen yet," he warned. "The principal could tell Mom no."

"But it's a plan." *Did you hear that, Phoenix? Your baby brother is getting a life!*

"After school—what will you do?" Zak asked me out of the blue.

"College, I guess." Not that I thought about my future. "Honestly, I get through each day, that's all."

He nodded. "Almost a year." He sighed.

"A year tomorrow." I plunged deep into my own worst fear. "And we still don't know. I think if we knew…a name, a clear picture…"

"You want me to help you out?"

"Zak, yes! Whatever you know, you have to share."

"OK. I was in the car with Phoenix. He stopped for gas." Slowly he ran through the events, pausing as if his memory jolted and skidded over certain details. "It was Friday night, the pumps were busy, Phoenix was running late. A guy on a Harley pushed into the line ahead of him. Phoenix didn't like that. He swore at the guy, and we switched lines, pulled up at the next pump alongside Nathan. Phoenix asked Nathan if he could step ahead of him in the new line."

"And Nathan was driving his Chevy, is that right?"

"I guess." Zak frowned with the effort of trying to remember.

"Was anyone in the car with him? Were Taylor and Jacob there?"

"Yeah, but not with Nathan. They were hanging out with some other kids from Forest Lake. Nathan was with Robert Black and Vince Hall. That was the day Hall sold Nathan the Chevy."

"OK, so Nathan tells Phoenix no way can he go ahead at the pump. Is there any chance that while they were having this conversation, either Black or Hall were trying to reclaim a forgotten stash of cocaine in Nathan's car? Is that what kicked off the fight in the first place?"

Instead of prodding his memory, my questions seemed to block Zak and his frown deepened. "Who told you that?"

"Nobody. It's a police theory. If these guys were arguing over a hidden drug stash, that could have caused things to turn violent. Is that what you saw?"

"If it happened, I didn't see it," he admitted, still looking blocked and confused.

I prompted again. "And maybe Brandon noticed what was happening from across the lot—guys starting to fight over drugs, with Phoenix and you both too close for comfort…"

"Back off!" Suddenly Zak stood up. "I don't want to talk about it anymore."

I drew a sharp breath, turned away then back again. "Try, Zak," I pleaded. "You were there. Give me a name, a reason…"

"No, you don't understand. I can't help you."

"Why not? What don't I understand?"

"Sure, I was there until Nathan and Phoenix got into their argument, then Brandon came over."

"And?"

"Brandon was yelling at Hall and Black—they were still near the Chevy. I didn't hear what he said. Then he turned and yelled for me to leave. He said—exact words, 'Get out of here, Zak—go home, now!'"

"And?" I said quietly, feeling my head spin and my heart thud with disappointment.

"I did—I ran away," he admitted. The kid had been living with this guilt for almost a year. "I did what Brandon told me, but I should've stayed."

"Why?" I murmured.

"To help my brother," he whispered back. "If I'd been there, I could've stopped it from happening. Phoenix would still be alive."

9

It's a big deal for Zak," Zoey said.

I'd gone from Michael's apartment to her house, knowing this was her day for physical therapy so she wouldn't be in school. I was interested in finding out what Russell Bishop knew about Nathan's arrest and how come he was so close to the police action, but first I had to share with someone what Zak had shared with me, and it was Zoey I chose. I'd found her in her covered arena, long reining one of her gray Arabian horses.

She sighed and shook her head. "The kid's only thirteen years old, and he believes he could have saved his brother."

"I told him—what chance would you have had? It was chaos, everyone had knives. He still said he should have been there for Phoenix."

For a while we watched Merlin trot, ears pricked, neck arched, high-stepping around the arena. "How perfect is he?" Zoey murmured. "You know, this is the first time I've put myself in Zak's shoes. I always look at him and judge him—moody kid, throwing his life away."

"That's the hard part," I admitted. "Seeing it the way other people see it. But I always felt a connection with Zak, and maybe with Sharon and Brandon, even when they hated my guts."

Zoey eased the pressure on Merlin and let him fall from trot into walk. He snorted then wandered toward us, looking for a reward. "How is it at home?" she asked.

"With moving? It's crappy. My whole life is tied up in black garbage bags."

"And the anniversary tomorrow—how are you doing?"

Six months ago, Zoey being kind to me would've brought on the desire to confess everything. *I have to tell you a secret—I visit Foxton Ridge. There's a barn and an old ranch house. I see Phoenix and the Beautiful Dead.* Hunter would've been there with the warning wings. These days, with time running out fast, I was over the sharing urge and my whole focus was on solving Phoenix's death. "I saw Kim Reiss," I told her instead. "It kind of works."

"She's cool. I like her."

"Me too."

"Did she do the pebble thing?"

"Yeah. A black lava stone for anger."

"I chose a piece of flint—sharp edges." For a moment she flashed back into the emptiness and rage of losing Jonas.

"What did you do with it?"

Zoey smiled. "I threw it out of the window. Kim said it was cool. How about you?"

"I put mine back. It's still in the bowl."

"Next time, throw it away—you'll feel better. Hey, and Phoenix would love it that you're taking care of Zak," Zoey told me, stroking Merlin's nose.

❦

I stayed and spent quality time with Zoey until her dad got back from golf. "Michael Rohr tells me you're on a mission to save Zak," he said when he found me and Zoey working the other horse, Pepper, in the arena. "You're doing a good job, Darina."

Wow! This was the first complimentary remark Russell Bishop had put my way—ever! "Thanks. But it's not me, it's everyone."

"It helps that Michael is back in Ellerton," Russell agreed, then led me in exactly the direction I wanted to go. "And good that Sheriff Kors is focused on cleaning up the town. Give the guy six months and we'll be back to where we were before."

He meant before kids started dying and everyone fell apart. But even Russell Bishop had the tact not to spell this out in front of Zoey and me.

"I heard he arrested Nathan Thorne?" I prompted.

"They charged him with possession of narcotics. Kors knows he's a small player, but you start with the little guys and move on up the food chain."

"Cool." Zoey and I echoed each other.

"Yeah, if I have one criticism, it's that they bailed Nathan out after they charged him. If it was down to me, I would lock up the lousy kid and throw away the key."

For once I agreed with the pillar of our community. How much better it would be if baby face Nathan was permanently off the scene…

"They released him?" Zoey was as shocked as I was.

Russell nodded. "They picked him up with only enough cocaine for personal use. The bottom line is—the sheriff hopes it will act as a warning and get Nathan to clean up his act. Personally, I doubt that." Looking at his watch, he cut the conversation short. "I'm out of here. You want a ride to your therapy?" he asked Zoey.

"No, thanks. I'll drive there."

"How about you, Darina? Can I drop you somewhere?"

"I have my car," I told him, pointing to where my shiny, red Brandon-mobile was parked.

"Nice vehicle," he muttered, raising an eyebrow, meaning, *Where did you get a car like that, Darina?* Then he went off to change out of his golf wear and meet his wife for an up-market lunch at the Blue Fin restaurant.

"How come Sheriff Kors is cozying up with your dad?" I asked Zoey as we led the horses into their stables.

"He knows Dad is considering running for mayor," she told me.

"Seriously?" I asked.

"Seriously," she said. And we both raised our eyebrows and grinned.

❧

I left the perfect setup—a house with air-conditioned stables and a white-columned portico, smooth lawns, electronically controlled gates—and drove into a nightmare.

I was through the gates, waving good-bye to Zoey, when I picked up the black Chevy in my overhead mirror. I saw three guys in the car and slammed my foot on the pedal, picked up speed along South 13th Street, and made a sharp right back toward town, hoping to lose them. No such luck—I had a crazy driver on my tail, taking the corner on two wheels, gaining on me as I sped past the medical center overlooking the park. By the time I reached the lights leading to the mall, they'd changed to red.

For a second I considered running the red light, but a truck crawled out of the side road, blocking my way. I slammed on my brakes, felt a jolt as the Chevy collided into me, saw the doors open and Nathan jump out along with bandana men, Hall and Black.

In a sedan I would have locked my doors, sat tight, and prayed. But this was a convertible, the top was open, and all the guys had to do was reach in and drag me out.

It happened in broad daylight, so sudden and fast that I was lifted out of my car before the truck had even turned the corner. No one else was around. I guess the truck driver was too busy to see the abduction or else he didn't want to get involved. I know no one called nine-one-one.

They gave Nathan the job of driving my car away from the junction. The other two gorillas wrestled me into the backseat of the Chevy, then one stayed with me, holding me down, while the other took the wheel and followed Nathan. They'd crashed into me, hauled me out of the convertible, and tossed me into their car, driven away, and the whole thing had lasted less than thirty seconds. That's how long it takes to kidnap someone and make them disappear.

I fought back the best I could. Either Black or Hall—I didn't know one from the other—put his hand around my throat and forced my head onto the floor so that I tipped out of sight and lay struggling for breath. Looking up into this guy's face, I saw narrowed eyes, a broad nose, dark stubble, and no sign that he meant to go easy on me. I gave up the fight and lay quiet. He eased his grip as the car picked up speed.

I was pinned to the floor of a beaten-up Chevy, surrounded by empty Doritos packages and silver gum wrappers, snatched off the street by three drug users who were driving me out of town to who knows what godforsaken destination. Life events don't come much worse than this.

"Hey, Vince, give me Nathan's sweatshirt," the guy with his boot on my spine growled.

Hall took one hand off the steering wheel, reached for a gray hooded jacket, and tossed it into the back. Black jerked at my arm, pulled me into a sitting position then muffled my face with the hood, securing it with the arms, which he tied in a knot around my mouth and neck. Afterward he scrabbled among the junk on the backseat, found another ligature, and tied my hands behind my back.

For the rest of the journey I was tightly gagged and blindfolded. My face sweated, it was hard to breathe, and I was seriously scared about what they planned to do next.

We drove for what felt like eternity.

Trussed up and stuffed into the well between the front and back seats, I tried to curl into fetal position—but every time Hall took a bend, I rolled and knocked my head or my shins. The motion—and sheer terror—made me nauseated.

"Are we almost there yet?" Robert Black said in a whiny, kiddie voice.

Hall laughed, said, "Five more minutes, honey," and roared the engine.

"When we get there, can we go swimming?" Black asked, still in his kid voice, though the word *swimming* came with a sinister emphasis.

"Maybe," Hall answered.

He swerved again, and I hit my head against a sharp metal edge. The hood over my mouth was wet with saliva. Clammy fabric covered my nose, my eyes, my ears.

"*Ta-dah*, we're here!" Hall announced at last.

Keeping the blindfold and gag in position, they cut the engine and dragged me out of the car, across some rough ground to a place where I could hear lapping water. Obviously, "swimming" was still on the agenda. A key turned in a lock, I was shoved up two steps, through a doorway, and into a musty corner where I lay curled on my side.

"Hey, Nathan." Black grunted a greeting.

"What took you so long?" Nathan answered.

"Your crappy car isn't built for speed, is what took us so long." As Hall answered, he stooped to untie the blindfold and lift the hood away from my face.

I blinked and kept my eyes screwed up, gradually making out a bare wooden floor, fishing rods leaning against a wall, two old folding chairs, and a dusty canvas bag hanging from a hook on the back of the door.

"*You* sold me the heap of shit," Nathan reminded him. "Darina doesn't know how lucky she is, driving her convertible."

The mention of my name brought Black's attention to the job at hand. He dragged me up from the floor and sat me on one of the chairs, making sure that my hands were still firmly tied. "Time for a swim?" he asked Nathan.

"No. We wait for my brother." The answer was casual, noncommittal.

"Oh, great!" Hall wasn't happy. He stood in the doorway looking out, rubbing his cheek then raising his shirt to scratch his rib cage. "Doesn't Oscar know I have better things to do than hang out in some crummy shack waiting for the cops to catch up with us?"

"The cops won't find us here," Nathan said evenly. "By the way, Robert, did you get Darina's cell phone?"

Black grunted, pushed me back in the chair, and went through my pockets. As soon as he found my phone, he switched it off, went to the door, and pitched it away. I heard the splash as it landed then sank.

"So spell it out—what exactly are we waiting for?" Hall insisted. He looked wired, clearing his throat and heading outside as Nathan sat in the other seat, legs sprawled.

"My brother would like to meet Darina face-to-face," Nathan said, giving me a nasty smile.

Gritting my teeth, I stared past him at the expanse of

smooth water visible through the doorway. In the distance I saw houses built into the hillside and recognized them as the million-dollar Forest Lake homes advertised on the local TV station. The lakeside shack we were in was tucked away off the main road, probably used only by weekend fishermen.

"You hear that, honey?" Black asked as he went to join Hall, who was re-tying the knot on his bandana as he leaned against my car. "The boss wants to meet you. I guess he plans to get out of you why you went to the cops and got Nathan arrested."

"I didn't. It wasn't me." When you're desperate, you lie. What else can you do?

"Sure it was you," Nathan cut in, tapping his foot against the floor and staring at me with those eyes that were slightly too big and round, sneering through the exaggerated cupid's bow of his lips. "You were rescuing Zak at the time, which by the way was a totally stupid idea. Zak's a Rohr—he can take care of himself. And it turns out my brother has Zak in his sights anyway."

I felt a fresh jolt of panic. "No. Whatever you think I did—Zak wasn't involved."

"He is now," Nathan told me, suddenly standing up and taking his phone out of his pocket. He turned his back and pressed a couple of buttons. "Hey, Oscar," he said. "We're ready for your visit."

This was the only chance I would get, I realized. Nathan's

back was turned, Hall and Black were outside, so, with my hands still tied behind my back, I sprang up from the chair and ran for the door, made it down the steps, and began to sprint away from the cars toward the dirt track.

I had roughly a three-second head start before Nathan yelled out a warning and Hall and Black saw where I was headed. They came hurtling after me, and there was never any doubt that they would catch me.

Hall was lighter and faster than Black. He grabbed the back of my shirt and flung me down, put a knee in my back, and waited for his buddy to join us. Then the two of them lifted me from the ground and carried me struggling back to the shack.

"This is why we don't wait for Oscar," Hall told Nathan, who stood in the doorway. His hooked arm stayed around my throat, while Black released my legs and set me upright roughly ten feet from the water's edge.

"My brother will be here in thirty minutes," Nathan promised. He'd started to look edgy, glancing down the dirt track and along the water's edge to check that there was no one nearby.

"That's thirty minutes too long," Hall grunted, keeping up the pressure on my throat.

"I'm with Vince," Black agreed. "If we're going to do it, we do it now."

They were older than Nathan. They'd been around the block more times, and Nathan knew it. "OK, but you two get your story straight for Oscar," he said, heading toward my car and jumping in. "I don't want to know."

"Yeah, Nathan, you don't know anything," Black mocked. "What are you going to do with the convertible?"

"I'll think of something."

"Drive it into the lake," Hall told him. "Then when they drag Darina's corpse out of the water, they'll figure it was an accident."

Hall's arm was around my throat, my hands were tied, and they were discussing my death. I had one of those whole-life-flashing-before-me moments—on vacation building sand castles with my dad, starting high school, seeing Phoenix the first time he walked down the corridor. Time slowed down. I envisaged my drowned body floating to the surface in the dawn light.

Nathan drove off without saying whether or not he would take their advice. Black stepped back in to help Hall, lifting me again and slinging me over one shoulder like a slab of meat, then stepping into the shallow water at the edge of the lake.

I kicked out hard, crashing my foot into his ribs. He waded on through the reeds until the water reached his waist then he slid me from his shoulder and tipped me on my back. I hit the water with an icy shock, sank under the surface, felt hands hold me down, looked up toward the glittering light. Pressing my lips tight together, clothes and hair floating around me, I kept on staring at the sun.

They pushed me down deeper. I saw their shadowy shapes above me, blocking out the light. Then suddenly, without warning, they let me go. I tilted my head and rose to the surface; my face broke clear. I gasped and breathed again.

And Phoenix was with me, surrounded by his halo of silver light, striking out at Black and throwing him backward deeper into the lake then turning on Hall, who put his arms over his head in a futile attempt to protect himself. Phoenix reached out, raised him, and hurled him onto the shore, ran after him and raised him again, sent him crashing to the ground where he lay senseless.

But now Black was emerging from the water, staggering through the reeds, ready to throw himself at Phoenix from behind.

Phoenix turned, his face expressionless. He caught Black in a rib-cracking bear hug and swung him around, then crashed him down on the ground beside Hall. The two lay groaning and covered in mud, battered and broken by Phoenix's superhuman strength.

He left them there and came back for me, lifted me out of the water and cradled me in his arms as he carried me to the shore. I felt the warmth of the sun on my skin, breathed clean air into my lungs. Arms around his neck, I clung to him as he strode away from the lake.

❧

"Believe me now?" Phoenix murmured as he drove me home in Nathan's old Chevrolet. His wet shirt clung to his chest and shoulders; water dripped onto his forehead and trickled down his cheeks. "Thorne and his guys won't stop until they're certain you're not a threat."

"Yes, and you'll be there to save me," I told him, refusing to admit how much my near-death experience had shaken me. Images of the sunlight quivering on the surface of the lake as I stared up from the depths stayed with me, and I still felt the pressure of Hall's arm around my throat.

Phoenix stopped the car on the hard shoulder. "Not always," he reminded me gently. "What happens after tomorrow—when I'm not here anymore?"

I shook my head and closed my eyes. "Don't. I don't want to think about it."

He sighed and shook his head. "Face it, Darina. By Friday I'll be gone. The Thornes will still be here, and they'll want to get even."

Forcing myself to look at him, I put on a brave face. "But by then we'll have got to the truth. We'll know the killer, and he'll be behind bars—end of story."

"Maybe," he said softly, not wanting to stray right now into the doubts and fears he'd already revealed. "Maybe not."

"We will. The more I get into this, the more I have Nathan as prime suspect. Right from the start, when Brandon put him there in the middle of things, I've had a creepy feeling."

"The kid's a sleazeball," Phoenix admitted, still noncommittal.

"And he has an army of older guys stopping us from finding out the truth—Oscar, Black, and Hall for starters. They all know he's guilty."

"That's my point." Frustrated, Phoenix did go back to his old argument. "That's exactly my point! They know, but they set up a barrier that no one can get through."

"So I go to Sheriff Kors," I decided. "I tell him they kidnapped me."

"No!" The strength of his reaction surprised me, and he fixed me with his stare. "If they arrest those four, you're safe for maybe twenty-four hours. After that, the entire drug cartel this side of the Rockies comes after you."

"Because I break the supply chain?"

"Yeah, you got it. So no arrests, OK?"

"OK." I couldn't argue—I didn't have the heart. "Stop looking at me like that, Phoenix. Just drive."

Reluctantly he put the car into gear. "Dean wants me back at Foxton," he told me as we drove past the fast-food joints on the Ellerton outskirts.

Dean, not Hunter, I thought with a sharp pang of regret.

"Dean does a good job," Phoenix insisted. "I'll discuss what just happened with him, get his reaction. I wish I didn't have to leave you," he added softly.

"I'll be OK," I told him.

"All I want to do is take care of you."

"You just did, remember?" Trying for a brave smile, all I achieved was a tiny upward curl of my lips.

Phoenix smiled back then kissed me. "Darina, I love you more every moment that passes," he whispered. "How is that possible?"

"Say that again!" I murmured, leaning in for another kiss. In the end it was Phoenix who pulled away. "Will you promise me you'll stay safe until tomorrow? Go home, eat, take a shower then sleep."

I knew I would never be able to sleep or eat, but I gave in on staying home. "I won't leave the house," I promised.

Please talk to me, let me in! I pleaded silently. He looked sadly at me, and I had a picture of him, a solitary figure standing on a small, deserted island—a black rock surrounded by a sea of despair. He didn't even raise his hand to wave good-bye.

Please!

With a small shake of his head he kept me out. "And at this point, Darina—however hard it feels, if Dean decides you should step back from this whole deal, you'll agree?"

And leave you drifting in eternal torment? Tears filled my eyes. *I'd rather die.*

"You won't have any choice," Phoenix murmured. "If the overlord says enough, Darina—you can't do any more, the Beautiful Dead will simply wipe your memory and leave."

10

"You're telling me you left your key in the ignition?"

This was Jim's eye-popping reaction when he heard my car had been stolen. It was Thursday morning, and he was just back from an overnight trip fixing software for an out-of-state winery.

"You know what day this is, so go easy on her," Laura warned. "It's a mistake anyone could make."

Jim wasn't listening. "Let me get this straight. You parked your car in the mall with the top down and the key in the ignition. You went shopping for shoes. When you got back, the car was gone."

"Yeah." That was the story I'd given Laura the night before, when she got back from work, by which time I'd thrown my wet clothes in the washing machine and taken a shower. "And I didn't even buy shoes. Dumb, huh?"

Jim shook his head slowly in disbelief. "Even for you, Darina."

"Listen, I don't care how it happened." The night before, Laura had immediately picked up the fact that I was extra fragile, put it down to the approaching anniversary, and held back from asking awkward questions. She'd taken on the job of calling the cops and reporting the theft. Now she moved in to protect me from my stepdad's inquisition, all the time wiping at kitchen surfaces with an antibacterial cloth. "So long as Darina wasn't in an accident, so long as she didn't get hurt—that's all I care about."

"Do you know how much that car is worth?" Jim asked, still incredulous. "And what are you going to do now? How will you get by without transportation? Do we even know if the insurance company will cover it?"

"I guess I can ask Brandon," I mumbled. *After Phoenix gets back to me with orders from the overlord. After I use Phoenix's last day on Earth to save my Beautiful Dead boyfriend from an eternity of doubt.* Any second now I was expecting a message from Foxton.

But it wouldn't come from the person who was at this moment pressing the doorbell.

"Who's that?" Jim shot me an accusing glance, as if the visit was connected with me and was bound to turn out bad.

"So now I can see through doors!" I snapped back. Laura let out an exasperated grunt, put down her cloth, and went to the door. She came back with Henry Jardine in uniform and holding up a set of car keys.

He smiled at me. "We recovered your vehicle, Darina."

"Good job, Henry!" Jim was quick with the compliments. "You guys work fast. Where did you find it?"

I was expecting an answer that involved Forest Lake and the whole car being submerged, waterlogged, and totally ruined. That would be fine by me—the cops would build a theory around opportunist thieves who took the car for a joyride before dumping it in the lake. There would be no fingerprints, no clues, no danger of Oscar Thorne's brother being implicated. But no.

"A security guy down at the Centennial industrial park called us early this morning. He was patrolling a unit where they manufactured furniture before cheap imports drove them out of business." Jardine had accepted Laura's silent offer of coffee and sat down at the kitchen table.

"I know the place," my stepfather acknowledged. "The Wonderful World of Wood—we bought a bed there in their closing sale." Typical get-the-facts-straight Jim.

My heart was sinking. *Stupid, badass Nathan! Why didn't you just drive the freakin' car into the lake, like Hall suggested?*

"The security guard drove around the back of the building, saw signs of forced entry, stepped inside, and found a forty-thousand-dollar stolen convertible parked inside a disused warehouse."

"So who would do something that dumb?" Jim asked while I hovered by the door, looking for a chance to leave.

"Some low IQ kid, huh?" So far Henry was enjoying himself. It isn't often a cop gets to deliver good news.

"Actually, we got clear fingerprints from the steering wheel, and they matched with a set we already have on file."

"Cool." Jim still approved.

But now Henry Jardine's expression grew more guarded. "At six o'clock this morning we were knocking on the door of Nathan Thorne, with an order for his arrest."

For me, the information was like the gates of the underworld opening up and letting out a pack of Oscar Thorne hellhounds. They would be at me again, dragging me down and tearing at my throat, and this time I got the sense that I wouldn't escape.

Laura picked up on my unease and came to stand next to me.

"We were out of luck—Nathan wasn't home," Jardine conceded. "He shares the house with his brother, Oscar, who wasn't happy about letting us in. We ignored him and tore the place apart—Nathan definitely did a disappearing act."

"But you're still out there looking for him?" Laura checked. "And you'll tell us the minute you find him?"

"We'll do that for sure." Jardine sipped his coffee and steered us back to what he thought was totally positive news. "This time we found a whole stash of class A drugs in Nathan's room, measured out, and ready to sell on the street," he continued. "We already built a case of illegal possession against the kid. After this, the charge sheet will read like an entire book."

Jim nodded. "I heard from Russell Bishop that Sheriff Kors was poised to clean up this town—seems he was right."

"Not only that," Jardine confided, enjoying himself again. "We found other prints besides Darina's on the car door, and again we came up with a clear match."

Laura saw I was shaking so much she actually took my hand and held it. "Are you going to give us names?" she asked.

"Yeah—they belong to two guys we've been gathering evidence on for a couple of years." The deputy sheriff was torn between the official line of not giving out classified information and the human temptation to share. "They're definitely in the frame for a serious traffic offense involving the death of a member of the county sheriff's police department."

By this time I felt so wound up and nauseated that I was hardly hearing what was said.

"Dean Dawson at Amos Peak," Memory Man Jim recalled swiftly. "You found those guys' prints on Darina's car?"

"Yeah, and at seven A.M. we sent teams out to pull them in. This time it worked out."

"Cool," Jim said, while Laura held on to my hand.

"Robert Black and Vincent Hall," Jardine said with slow,

steady emphasis, staring right at me. "Right now they're safe behind bars in the sheriff's office, and no way will we unlock the door before they go before the judge."

✦✦✦

I didn't get my car back right away—the forensic officers held it to take pictures and consolidate their evidence—so I set out for Center Point on foot, planning to bring Zak into the loop so he knew Nathan was still on the loose—mad, bad, and dangerous as could be.

I wanted to warn Zak to be on his guard, but I hadn't reached the end of my street before I felt Laura draw up beside me.

"Where are you going?" she leaned out and asked.

"Nowhere. Just walking."

"Why don't you stay home?"

"Because!" I muttered, guessing Laura was on her way to work and didn't have time for a long heart-to-heart.

"I don't want you out on the streets—not until Henry tells us that they've got Nathan Thorne."

I nodded and crouched beside her car. "OK, I'll go visit Zoey or Hannah—whoever's home. I'll take care."

"Let me drive you there," she begged.

"No, Mom—it's cool."

"Then you get behind the wheel," she decided, making me step back as she got out of the car and walked around to the passenger side. "You drive me to work and keep the car for the day. That way I can breathe a little easier."

"Deal," I agreed. I drove to the mall, dropped her off outside the clothing shop where she worked, said good-bye, and doubled back in the direction of Michael Rohr's place.

So I'd parked Laura's dark blue sedan near the tower block entrance, next to an old, black Chevrolet, and walked as far as the elevator shaft, pressing the button for the second floor before I realized the significance of "old black Chevrolet." My stomach flipped, and when the elevator whined and the doors slid open, I was expecting to see Nathan Thorne walk out with Zak hooded, bound, and gagged.

But actually the elevator was empty, and I had enough time to backtrack in my mind to the evening before, when Phoenix had driven me in Nathan's Chevy to the outskirts of town.

"I can't come any farther in case someone sees me," he'd told me as he parked in a lot outside Blockbuster. "You walk straight home, stay inside, and wait there for me."

I'd promised again that I would and, taking care that there was no one around, Phoenix had done his shimmery dissolving act. I'd gone home, showered, invented a convincing story for Laura about the theft of my convertible, and so far done exactly as Phoenix had told me—sit tight, wait—until Deputy Sheriff Jardine had knocked on our door.

So what had happened since then to bring the Chevy from the parking lot outside Blockbuster to Center Point?

A quick figuring out painted the picture in my mind that someone—some aimless kid ready to poke his nose into other people's business—had called Nathan late last night to ask him if he was out of gas, or else why was his car dumped in an out-of-town lot, and did he need a ride out there to collect it? Which would put Nathan back behind the wheel, driving here to see Zak, which also meant that I was right—Nathan could be here with Zak right now.

As I stood thinking this through, the door closed and the elevator whined upward, clunked, and shuddered to a stop.

What would Nathan do to Zak if he found him?

"This is so not good," I muttered to myself as the elevator whined, clunked, and shuddered down once more.

"Hey, Darina," Michael Rohr said to me as he stepped out. He seemed chilled and relaxed, wearing a two-day stubble and a crumpled linen shirt.

I eased back on my concerns and returned the greeting. "Hey, Michael. Is Zak at home?"

"That kind of depends on your interpretation of the word *home*. Do you mean here, or his mom's house?"

"Here. I need to talk with him." I didn't say why or fill

Michael in on the latest details connected with Nathan, Hall, and Black. I didn't tell him that since the last time we met I'd been half drowned in Forest Lake and was worried they might try something similar on his youngest son.

"Sorry, it seems like Zak's a popular guy. A couple of buddies already called."

"He went out? Who with?"

"I have no clue. That was before Brandon showed up. I told him the same story—Zak went out early."

"Brandon was here, too?"

Michael pursed his lips. "You have a lot of questions, Darina. It seems Zak hasn't made any final decision about where he wants to stay, so Sharon sent Brandon over with a bag of clean clothes."

"And this other kid—you don't know his name, but what did he look like?" The black Chevy in the parking lot still loomed large, and I was pressing for answers.

"I didn't get a clear view. Zak answered the door. What is this—the third degree?"

"No, everything's cool. I was just curious."

"I only saw the kid from the window. I guess that's his car," Michael said and pointed to the Chevy.

That was it—my fears were confirmed. "Long, black hair, kind of baby faced?" I asked.

"That's him. He was getting into the car with Zak when

an older guy in a black Mercedes pulled up. Zak and his buddy changed their minds and got into the Mercedes instead. Nice set of wheels—who can blame them?"

"OK, thanks." I nodded and turned, started to run toward Laura's car.

"Is everything OK?" Michael called after me. "What happened to your convertible?"

"It got stolen. Yeah, everything's cool!" I yelled back, my mind in chaos as I reached the car.

I should have stayed, told Michael the full story—I know that now.

❧

My first thought was to ignore Phoenix's instructions and drive straight out to Foxton. That would be forty-five minutes, maybe an hour in Laura's car. Was that better than going to Henry Jardine? How would the cops react when they heard Nathan Thorne had visited Center Point and his car was still there? Would they step up their search?

I drove aimlessly, trying to fix on my next move.

Jeez, Darina, tell someone! Arizona-in-my-head came back full volume. *You know how it feels to be snatched off the street. Do something, for Christ's sake!*

"OK, I go back and tell Michael," I said, doing a U-turn.

No way. Zak's dad already left, my internal Arizona reminded me. *Who knows where he is now?*

"So it's the cops." I swung back around, across a line of traffic.

Or Sharon? Arizona reminded me. *If my kid had been kidnapped, I'd want to know.*

"I can't get my head around this." I groaned. "Phoenix, what do I do?"

There was no answer.

Try to stay calm, Summer would say. I listened hard for her voice from beyond the grave. *Who knows the reason Nathan went to Michael's apartment? Maybe Zak is safe after all.*

I shook my head. "He's in trouble. I have to do something."

I stopped at a red light, and Brandon pulled up beside me carrying a passenger.

"Zak needs us!" I gasped.

The passenger was Kyra, the gas station cashier, looking cute in a fringed jacket and leather pants on the backseat of a Harley—but this wasn't the point. I didn't realize she knew Brandon this well, is all I'm saying.

Brandon pointed across the street to a KFC parking lot.

"Follow me," he said.

By the time I parked next to him, Kyra had got off the Dyna and disappeared. "What car does Oscar Thorne drive?" I asked Brandon, who had dismounted and was staring at me, trying to decide if I was nuts.

"Mercedes," he told me.

"Black?"

He nodded.

"OK, so Oscar and Nathan have got Zak."

"You're certain?"

"Yesterday they snatched me from my car. They tried to kill me."

"Slow down. Breathe. What's that got to do with them taking my brother?"

"Oscar knows I told the cops Nathan was carrying drugs. He also knows Zak was there and that I hang out with Zak. Now the cops are after Nathan. They already arrested Black and Hall."

"Again, breathe." Brandon's eyes narrowed. He looked as if he was going to waste time yelling at me then changed his mind. "Deep breaths, Darina. Think. Do you know where they would take Zak?"

"They drove me out to Forest Lake. I don't think they would do the same thing twice. And they wouldn't take him to their house, not with the cops crawling all over the place."

"Somewhere out of town?" Brandon prompted.

"Foxton maybe?"

"No. Why Foxton?"

"I just thought maybe."

"Not Foxton," I insisted, thinking, *Phoenix, where are*

you? Dean, get someone down here fast! "But there's a place out on the Forest Lake road, a trailer park, where the kids hang out."

"I know it." He swung his leg over the saddle and told me to take Kyra's place. "You'd better be right, Darina," he said as he started the engine. "And you pray that we get there in time!"

The Dyna swept out of town, past the fast-food joints lining the entrance to the interstate. Brandon leaned into the bends until our knees almost scraped the asphalt, soared up the hills, over the brows, and down into the dips with gut-churning speed. I crouched behind Brandon's broad frame and held on tight.

The sign told us that Forest Lake was eight miles ahead. "We're almost there!" I yelled at Brandon as the wind tore the words from my mouth. "See the trailers on your left—slow down!"

He eased off the accelerator, and the world regained focus. I took a deep breath. "That's the one—up ahead."

Brandon stopped the bike fifty yards from the derelict trailer. Through the tall pine trees we made out a vehicle parked on the far side of the trailer, the sun glinting on the windshield and bouncing off the sleek bodywork of a black Mercedes.

"Oscar Thorne!" I whispered.

Quiet! Brandon raised a warning finger to his lips, got off the bike, and crept forward through the trees. For a big guy he moved smoothly and silently, crouching slightly and taking care not to crack fallen twigs underfoot. I held my breath and followed.

Ahead, I made out familiar details of the dull silver trailer—the small, grimy windows, the door with the smashed pane of glass, the metal steps kicked carelessly to one side. And I pictured the scene inside of Zak with his hands tied behind his back, a gag across his mouth, with the Thorne brothers taking their time, taunting him, telling him exactly the way it would end.

Twenty paces away, Brandon stopped. He listened to every sound—the flap of a blue jay's wings as it rose from a tree overhanging the trailer, the hum of traffic on the interstate, the breeze rustling through the pine branches overhead. Meanwhile, I was picking up a sharp smell that penetrated my nostrils and hit the back of my throat—recognizing it as the smell of gasoline.

Brandon smelled it, too, and after a while he jerked his head in the direction of the parked Mercedes and made his way around the back of the trailer.

We skirted carefully between the trees, upwind of the smell and along a ledge of rock behind the trailer then came down again a few feet from the car, where we crouched low. *What now?* I mouthed at Brandon.

He signaled for me to stay in hiding behind the Mercedes while he crept forward to look in through the nearest window. I watched him do it, my hands balled into fists, hardly breathing. He reached the trailer, cupped his hand to the window to cut out his reflection, and peered inside.

"Hey, you must be Darina," a voice hissed at me from behind. "I'm Oscar Thorne. Happy to meet you at last."

This was one of those moments when everything happens faster than you can tell it, yet the whole of time seems to slow down and the adrenaline pumping through your system gives everything crystal clarity.

Oscar Thorne said hey and clamped his evil-smelling hand over my mouth. He'd been handling a can of gas—the stench came off his skin and filled my lungs. Brandon peered in through the trailer window, and the door flew open. Out came baby face Nathan, carrying a weapon—a small, gray gun—snug in his hand. He ran around the side of the trailer and held it straight at Brandon's head.

Brandon stood as still as a statue, the barrel of the gun pressed to the spot between his eyebrows. Oscar kept his hand to my mouth and shoved me out from behind the car. I made a strangled cry.

Nathan held his arm braced and the gun in position. He glanced at Oscar for instruction.

"Take care of the girl," Oscar ordered as he released me and sent me staggering toward them. "Give me the matches." With his free hand Nathan felt in his jeans pocket then tossed the box to his brother, who caught it and strode on toward the trailer. As I fell against Brandon, he steadied me and gave me a look that said, *Do nothing. Don't move! Don't scream!*

"Oh, by the way," Oscar said, pausing in the doorway and rattling the box of matches toward us. He allowed us a glimpse inside, where we could make out Zak's body slumped motionless on the floor. "We were planning to torch this rusting pile of crap—we soaked it with gas, ready to watch the baby burn. Then you two showed up without an invitation, to make the event even sweeter."

Brandon's gaze flicked from the trailer to Nathan, who held the gun steadily in position. As Nathan took his eye off Brandon to watch Oscar open the box, take out a match, and strike a light, Brandon exploded into action.

He swiped his fist up toward the gun and knocked it clean out of Nathan's hand. I flung myself on top of it and lay there while Nathan tried to kick and drag me clear, leaving Brandon free to run at Oscar, who threw the lighted match into the trailer.

There was a whoosh and a burst of bright orange flame inside the doorway, which I saw through the blows that Nathan was inflicting. Oscar took a step back from the force of the flames, and Brandon thrust him to one side, heaved himself up the trailer steps, and disappeared inside.

I fumbled for the gun, grabbed it in my right hand, rolled onto my back, and aimed it at Nathan with my finger around the trigger. I rose slowly to my feet.

"She's got the gun!" Nathan yelled to Oscar, his face crumpling, his whole body starting to shake.

Oscar backed away from the burning trailer, turned, and started to run toward us until I swung the gun and aimed at his head. He stopped suddenly.

"Don't come any nearer!"

I was shaking more than Nathan. Could I do it? Could I actually pull the trigger? I couldn't bear the picture that flashed into my head of a bullet exploding inside Oscar's skull—a bullet that I had fired. Still I pointed the gun and warned him to stay back.

Behind Oscar a wall of fire blazed in the trailer doorway. Black smoke billowed into the air. Seconds seemed like an eternity. Here we were—a sheet of flames, a cloud of smoke, and me with a gun in my hand facing two guys who wanted to kill me.

Then Brandon broke out of the trailer. He'd flung his

own jacket over Zak's head and carried him out on his shoulder, emerging from the flames like a figure out of the jaws of hell.

"Grab the gun!" Oscar yelled at Nathan.

Nathan made his move. I fired over his head. It turned out I couldn't shoot to kill. The shot cracked, the bullet missed. I kept on firing my warning shots—once, twice, three times. Nathan jumped sideways, yelped, and ran off through the trees. I turned the gun on Oscar. Behind him, Brandon lowered Zak to the ground, bent down, and listened to his chest.

"Is he breathing?" I called, hating the gun in my hand and the way it kicked and leaped when I fired. I kept it aimed at Oscar Thorne's head.

Brandon nodded and raised himself to his feet, his face blackened by smoke.

I aimed and stared at Oscar—he had the same bulging eyes as Nathan, but a meaner face, a harsher mouth. His dark hair was shaven close to his head. He stared back at me, small muscles flicking in his jaw, his eyes calculating the chances of me firing another shot.

"One move and I shoot!" I hissed.

His eyes narrowed. *I don't believe you!*

"I will—I'll shoot to kill!"

Shaking his head, Oscar took two steps toward his car.

Another step and he was opening the door and getting in. He slammed the door and turned the ignition.

My hand shook so hard that my finger slid from the trigger.

Oscar put his foot on the accelerator and drove away. With a groan of self-disgust I threw down the gun and ran to Brandon and Zak. Brandon leaned back his head and sucked in air. On the ground, Zak turned his head sideways and coughed. His eyes flickered open.

Behind us the trailer was an inferno. Heat cracked the windowpanes and buckled the metal walls, flames burst out, the black cloud gathered between the branches of the trees. Falling to my knees, I held Zak's head and told him he was going to be OK. He looked up at me, tried to sit, but slumped back down. I wiped the streaks of soot from his face. "Brandon saved you," I murmured. "He didn't care about himself. He just went in there and carried you out. In my whole life I never saw anything so brave!"

11

After the trailer fire the Rohrs closed ranks. I was there when the paramedics arrived to treat Zak for smoke inhalation and minor burns, but after I got a ride into Ellerton in the back of Sheriff Kors's car, I had no contact with Brandon. I gave my version of events to Kors then went straight to Michael's apartment, which was empty. Then I went to Sharon's house where Brandon opened the door. He'd already showered and changed his clothes.

"How's Zak doing?" was my first, anxious question.

"They're keeping him in the hospital overnight. Mom and Dad are there with him."

"But he's going to be OK?"

A slight nod was all I got. Brandon obviously had no plan to invite me in.

"What's wrong?" I asked the hero of the hour. "What did I do?"

His hostile look intensified as he stepped out of the house and closed the door behind him. "Darina, you don't have to *do* anything. You just *are*."

"Am what?"

"Trouble. It follows you, sticks around like a bad smell."

"Didn't I just help save Zak?" I was shaken and still torn apart by the fact that I'd let Nathan and Oscar escape, trying to make sense of Brandon's negativity.

"And would they have even thought about trying to kill him without you stepping in where you're not wanted?" he pointed out.

"I wasn't…I didn't mean…"

"I…I…I…This isn't about *you*, Darina." Brandon sat me down forcefully on the bench under the kitchen window. "Last time we spoke, we decided you were grown up enough to take care of yourself without my help. Even though it turns out that's not true, it was still my way of saying thanks but no thanks—I want you out of our lives."

"That's not fair," I pleaded.

"Sure it is—for all the reasons you already know." Sitting on the doorstep beside the bench, Brandon rested his arms on his bended knees. "Number one—it's hard for Mom to look at you without blaming you for Phoenix."

"Not anymore. We talked. Everything's cool."

He spoke over me, drowning me out. "Two—whatever you do turns bad. Today Zak almost died."

"Yeah, and without me he would still be hanging out

with Taylor Stafford and Jacob Miller, spending time with drug addicts like Black and Hall. He'd most likely be in jail!"

"Better there than dying in a trailer fire."

I gasped and stopped. Brandon really meant what he said.

"Go figure, Darina—this obsession with finding Phoenix's killer will end in someone else dying. Look what you unleashed—from now until the cops find the Thorne brothers, I can't let Zak out of my sight."

"Kors will catch them," I swore. "And today is the anniversary. How come your family isn't involved in this with me, chasing every lead, talking to witnesses, putting pressure on guys who were there—those people who know stuff that they're not saying?"

"Because!" Brandon spread his palms upward but refused to go over old ground. "Darina, if you want to keep on being a one-woman army on a mission to root out evil, whatever it is you're doing and for whatever reason, you go ahead. But leave us out of it." Jab, jab, jab with his forefinger—Brandon gave six jabs for every word in the last sentence then he stood up and opened the door.

"You don't talk to me, to Zak, to any of us ever again!" He stepped over the threshold. *Bang!* The door slammed behind him.

So, Phoenix, your brother won't help me find your killer.

And where were you, out at the trailer park? What's your new overlord's take on this? Does he know the cops got Hall and Black? Is he pleased? Does anyone even care?

I was dazed as I got in Laura's car and drove to the gas station, doing things on automatic pilot, only knowing that I was alone and time was racing on. Why the gas station? Kyra was the reason—her name popped into my head with two unanswered questions: how well did she know Brandon Rohr, and why hadn't she disclosed their friendship during our earlier conversation?

Luckily—or unluckily—she was working a shift behind the cash register when I arrived. This time she was busy filing her nails.

"I came to tell you Brandon's OK," I began. "I knew you'd be worried."

Kyra gave a lip gloss pout. "Brandon's a big boy."

"He saved Zak's life."

Surely this would drag her attention away from her manicure. But no—*sst-sst-sst* went the emery board.

"Oscar Thorne set fire to the trailer. Brandon ran right in and carried his brother out."

"Quite the hero." She perched on the edge of her seat, legs crossed, poured into her shiny leather pants.

"You didn't tell me you two knew each other," I reminded her. The time she talked to me, she'd left out Brandon's name until I'd brought it in. "What's not to notice?" she'd asked, like she admired him from a distance.

Only at that point had she remembered that Nathan ran at Brandon with a piece of heavy pipe and knocked him to the ground.

Kyra flicked the emery board across her nail one last time. She pressed a button to activate one of the gas pumps out front and watched as the customer filled his tank.

"What happened after Nathan hit Brandon?" I asked. "After Brandon hit the deck?"

"It was a year ago." She sighed. "You think I can remember every detail?"

"You could try!" I said, leaning over the desk and letting my feelings show.

Kyra was my last shot at getting the necessary information. After this I hit an unclimbable brick wall.

"Why would you *not* want to help me?"

"Because look what just happened to Zak," she said, right in my face so that I saw every individual, curled mascara-lash. She was staring at me, perhaps with a hidden warning that I wasn't able to read. "You want me to end up as toast?"

I stared her out. "Back to the day it happened. Brandon's on the ground, Nathan's standing over him. Black, Hall, Oscar Thorne—they all arrive on the scene. Who pulls the first knife?"

There seemed to be a long pause, and I never did get an answer because, at this exact moment, Oscar and Nathan Thorne burst out of the storeroom behind Kyra's desk.

And again at that precise second, between the shelves of potato chips and Snickers bars, Phoenix, Iceman, and Dean suddenly appeared.

⁂

The Beautiful Dead got me out of there before the Thornes could rush past Kyra and grab me. In broad daylight, in front of witnesses they cast the shimmering light and vanished me, took me out to Foxton in the blink of an eye.

"People saw you!" I gasped. I was in the ranch house with Iceman, coming to terms with the fact that they'd surrounded me with that magic glow and transported me through space. For this, don't think *kerpow* supersonic speed—think floating, spinning, hazy free fall. One second I was eyeballing Oscar and Nathan at the gas station, the next I was sitting in the rocking chair at the ranch—and what happened in between I didn't really get. "You're not allowed to let far-siders know you exist!" I stressed.

Iceman nodded. "That's how come Dean and Phoenix had to stay behind to deal with them," he explained quietly.

"They'll do the memory zap thing on the Thornes and Kyra?"

"Yeah, and those guys will wake up with sore heads and no clear idea of what just happened. So for them, what's new?"

I raised my eyebrows at Iceman's warped sense of humor. "This is so not funny!"

"I agree—it's serious. That's why Dean decided we should step in. After yesterday at Forest Lake and today at the trailer park, he couldn't risk those guys getting hold of you again."

"Your overlord has been monitoring my progress?" I queried, sounding calm and trying to stamp down my inner turmoil.

"Or lack of it." Iceman didn't pretty things up—he told it like it was. "You know, I'm starting to see things Phoenix's way. I figure there was total chaos there the night he was killed—too many guys, too many weapons. The cops have tried and failed, so what real hope do you have of finding his killer?"

"And Dean—does he see it that way, too?" This was the big question that everything else hung on.

Iceman heard noises outside and went to the window.

"Ask him yourself," he told me, pointing to two figures striding across the yard.

Dean was the first to enter. He flung open the door and looked at me long and hard with that stony overlord gaze.

Phoenix stood behind him on the porch.

"Don't listen to Phoenix and Iceman," I began, springing from the chair and running toward Dean. "This is our last day. Give me one more chance!"

Dean's gaze intensified and stopped me in my tracks.

Then he glanced over his shoulder, stood to one side, and let Phoenix come into the kitchen. "Take all the time you need," he told him, like a doctor who has just delivered a killer diagnosis and who recognizes that the patient might need help to adjust.

Phoenix took me by the hand and led me out of the house, across the yard, and through the meadow where the green grass grew tall and the scarlet poppy petals drooped and dropped. A fresh breeze blew down from the aspen ridge.

"Why does this feel like giving in?" I whispered, my heart filling with dread.

"Listen to me," he murmured, keeping hold of my hand and walking on. "I will not let this happen. I will *not* let you get killed."

"Don't think about me!" I begged. "Think about you. Today is all you have!" *All we have!*

Phoenix's grip strengthened. His fingers were laced through mine—his were ice-cold, mine were warm. "We can't trust the cops to arrest the Thornes," he insisted.

"Yes, you can. Kors is good at his job. He'll track them down."

"Not soon enough."

On we went, out of the meadow, across the thorn scrub and flat slabs of glittering pink rock, up the hill toward the water tower.

"I've told Dean this is it, we're out of here," Phoenix murmured in the shadow of the tower. "It's my choice, and it's a straight one—your life or mine. It's a no-brainer."

I made him turn and look right at me, deep into my eyes. "I did this three times before—for Jonas, Arizona, and Summer. I can do it again."

He'd cut himself off from me and made up his mind.

"No, Darina, you can't. This time it's Oscar Thorne we're dealing with."

"This time it's you," I countered.

He looked at me so long, so deep that I thought the silence would go on forever. We were still in the shadow of the tower, beneath the canopy of bright green aspen leaves, with the sweep of the mountains behind us, the blue sky above.

Phoenix, my Phoenix, I won't stop now. I'll never give in.

"I don't want you to grieve for me," he said softly as the breeze blew his hair from his face, revealing the angle of his cheekbones and jawline, the curve of his eyebrows, the depth of those blue-gray eyes.

As long as I breathe I'll grieve for you. You're in my head, my heart—you always will be. How can I kill the memories?

Why would I want to?

"But don't be sad. Be happy."

All I want is more time with you.

We walked on hand in hand toward Angel Rock.

"We'll have more time together, but it'll be different," Phoenix said.

"How—different?" The word scared me. *I want it to be the same.*

We stopped, and he turned toward me. "You believe in the soul? I don't mean any special religion—just the idea of a spirit."

I think I do.

"An energy, a life force, and we're all part of it. It's where we come from and where we go to."

Turning again and walking me toward Angel Rock, he held my hand so firm, looked so deep into my innermost thoughts, that I said out loud, "Yes, I believe that."

"I'm part of that energy and so are you. That's how I get to be there with you next week when you're back in school, next year when you go to college, when you party and dance—I'll be there."

I believe you.

"I'll be there when you meet the right guy and raise your kids. And whatever I said in the past, I promise I won't be jealous—I'll be happy for you."

I understand. My heart was squeezed. I could hardly breathe.

"At all your life events I will be by your side."

Now my heart was aching, bursting, breaking. I held on to his cold, cold hand.

"I will watch you grow old," he promised.

❖❖❖

"I know one thing for sure," Dean announced. It was late afternoon, and the shadows in the yard were long and deep.

"We have a situation with the Thorne brothers that makes it too dangerous to send Darina back."

"So we quit," Phoenix insisted. "How many times do I need to say it?"

I shook my head. "I won't. I can't."

Dean turned to Phoenix to explain my point of view.

"You see what Darina's saying? If she quits now, that's it for her—she won't be able to move on with her life. What kind of future does she have, knowing that she failed in the most important task she ever had?"

"Thanks." I sighed. "Make him understand, tell him we don't have time to talk—we need to move on."

Deep in thought, Dean led the way into the barn, where Iceman sat quietly on the steps leading to the hayloft. He was resting, recharging his powers, waiting for the overlord's decision.

"Go sit, Darina," Dean told me, and I went to the steps and sat down next to Iceman. Somehow, his quiet presence and the big dark space soothed me, like being next to a priest in an empty church.

Dean stood with Phoenix near the door. "My decision is that we go on," he told him calmly. "But Darina stays here with us."

I took a breath, deep and slow. *We go on!*

Phoenix gazed at me across the floor of the barn. *I love you, Darina. I will not let you die.*

"I know this looks like chaos," Dean went on. "But we need to establish some logic, some pattern. What happened before the fight at the gas station? What key facts are we missing here?"

I admired Dean's cop brain, at work on motives, moving toward opening a new line of inquiry. "Like, why did Nathan hit Brandon?" I asked eagerly. "What reason did he have?"

Dean nodded and turned to Phoenix. "Was there something in the background—a key detail that we overlooked?"

"Nothing that I know of." Phoenix sounded defeated. "My brother doesn't talk about stuff like that."

"But he's part of the culture," Dean pointed out. "He hangs with guys who know the Thornes. He listens and picks up information."

"Brandon isn't into drugs." Phoenix came back with more force to defend his brother.

"That's what I figured. I'm not saying he was part of the deal. But focus on exactly that fact—Brandon isn't part of the Thornes' organization, but he knows their lifestyle.

"Plus, he's a guy who can take care of himself—you don't push Brandon Rohr around."

"You're certain Brandon never shared any information with you about Oscar and Nathan Thorne?" I checked with Phoenix. "Or about any of that gang—Black or Hall?

"Or what about the younger kids, Stafford and Miller?"

"We didn't talk," he insisted. "That's the way it was."

"So—Oscar Thorne has his Ellerton territory." Dean moved us on. "Believe me, I know—this is a specific area, with established boundaries. Deals are done. Drug mules link the international runners with the local chief. A lot of guys know how it works and who works it, but no one says they know or does anything to challenge the system."

"But maybe Brandon did," I suggested. "What if he saw his kid brother hanging out with Stafford and Miller and knew that Zak was getting pulled into some nasty stuff—wouldn't he act on that?"

"Most guys would," Iceman agreed, and we all looked at Phoenix for his reaction.

He stood silent for a while, his face pale and thoughtful while the bond of family loyalty took hold. "You're guessing," he said. "You can never be sure."

"Which is why we get to travel back in time," Dean decided, standing between two narrow shafts of light in the gloomy barn. "We take a look at a couple of things and establish a motive. We move on from there."

I have wings, and I'm spinning through a black tunnel. I don't know which way is forward and which way is back. Gravity doesn't exist, only a pinprick of light that we move toward, which I glimpse then lose. A terrible force is dragging, twisting, propelling me on. Phoenix and Dean are with me, their white wings folded, helplessly turning, tumbling, whirling through space.

The speck of light grows to a disc. We fall and spin in pain toward it. The force tears at our limbs, our clothes, and hair.

We spiral on, the light expands, brilliant and blinding. I close my eyes and open my wings. The agony ends. We are there.

Angel-me stands invisible beside Dean and Phoenix in a huge, cold, empty warehouse with sleet rattling down on the metal roof. There are no windows, no electric light, and for a while we see nothing.

We hear the muffled sound of a car engine pull up outside the building and cut out. A door opens, and daylight floods in.

We're surrounded by hundreds of large, square objects covered in see-through plastic wrapping, taped up, ready for transportation. Beneath the wrapping I make out tables and chairs, beds and sofas. The big sticky labels on the outside read: The Wonderful World of Wood.

Oscar Thorne and Vince Hall lead the way between the unwieldy humps of packaged furniture that look like lumbering prehistoric creatures toward a small glass office in the corner. Nathan Thorne follows close behind, calling to Jacob Miller and Zak Rohr to keep up.

"There's no one here," he assures them. "The business went bust two weeks before Christmas."

Jacob looks scared but excited, Zak just plain scared.

I glance sideways at Phoenix, see him take a step toward Zak before Dean reaches out a hand to stop him.

"There's not a thing you can do to change things," Dean says.

"Zak shouldn't be here," Phoenix mutters. "He knows not to hang out with these people."

Dean frowns, communicates a telepathic warning, and makes Phoenix focus on the action.

"I said, it's OK!" Nathan insists. He comes so close to us we could reach out and touch him, waiting right there for the others to catch up. "What's with you guys?" he mutters. "You know you don't make my brother wait."

Angel-me spreads my wings and rises into the air with

Dean and Phoenix, who's staring down at Zak, trying to read his state of mind. We go ahead to the glass office, where we see Oscar and Vince placing dozens of small packages in rows on the desk. Vince begins to count and rearrange the packages, while Oscar looks out impatiently through the glass partition.

Nathan and Jacob hurry toward the office. Zak hangs back.

Then we hear another engine approaching. This time it sounds like a motorbike. The screech of tires tells us that it has pulled up in a hurry.

Oscar hears it, leans over the desk, and with his forearm sweeps the packages into a leather sports bag. Vince leaps up, breaks out of the office, and begins to sprint down the aisle of furniture toward the door. Nathan, Jacob, and Zak stay rooted to the spot.

I hover over the action with the Beautiful Dead.

Before Vince reaches the exit, Brandon appears, silhouetted against the light. Behind him is a curtain of sleet that slants toward the ground and a million tiny white balls rebound.

Invisible Phoenix lets out a groan as his older brother shows up. He's desperate to step in again and is hurting big-time because he knows he can't.

Vince sees Brandon and hesitates. Back in the office, Oscar closes the zipper on the bag and comes out with it tight under his arm. Brandon strides toward Vince, who comes at him, but Brandon lands the first punch, which sends him crashing into the furniture. Without saying a word, Brandon walks on, takes hold of Zak's arm, turns him toward the door, and starts to march him out of the building.

Twenty paces away, Nathan sets off after Brandon and Zak.

He takes a shortcut, vaulting over tables, shoving chairs aside, and overtaking the Rohrs before they have a chance to reach the door. Pulling a knife from his pocket and setting himself across their path, he stands with his feet wide apart, eyes staring wildly.

Brandon says nothing, only looks irritated at the interruption. He glances over his shoulder at Oscar, who is pulling Vince Hall free of the furniture, then at Miller, suddenly looking like he wishes he wasn't there. "Ttt." Brandon makes a clicking noise with his tongue then gestures for Zak to step to one side. He stares at the knife in Nathan's hand and sighs.

"You lay a finger on him and you're dead!" Oscar warns Brandon.

The threat brings a frown to Brandon's face. Again he's irritated.

Oscar's voice rises an octave. "No shit—you're dead!"

"Ttt." Brandon lashes out at Nathan, sends the knife clattering to the ground and Nathan staggering back through the doorway where he skids on the sleet-covered ground, loses his balance, and lands hard.

"Walk!" Brandon orders Zak, shoving him through the door.

Zak also staggers, almost tripping over Nathan, who squirms on the ground.

Brandon picks up the weapon. As he strides past Nathan, he treads hard on the hand that grasped the knife. Then Brandon and Zak walk out of sight.

"I swear—he's a dead man," Oscar mutters, hearing Nathan yell out and setting off after Brandon.

Hall hooks an arm around Oscar's waist to hold him back.

"Not now," he tells him, tapping the bag containing the drugs to remind him of important business. "Later."

Oscar tries to break free. "I'll get the kid, too," he promises his little brother, who has crawled on all fours back into the warehouse.

"Later!" Hall insists.

Outside in the whiteout world, we hear a motorbike roar to life. Hovering in the dark roof space of the Wonderful World of Wood, I watch the scene play out then look at Phoenix's troubled face.

"How do you feel?" I ask him, trying hard to imagine how I would react right now in his shoes.

He doesn't answer, just holds up his hand to ask me not to speak and let the scene play out.

"Leave it to me—I'll get Zak!" Nathan argues it out with Oscar, keeping his injured hand pressed to his chest. His baby *face is flushed with shame. "No one walks away from this— not Zak Rohr, not Brandon, nobody!"*

❧

The journey back to the present hurts just as much as traveling into the past. Every muscle is twisted, every joint feels like it's being wrenched apart. You enter the vortex, and it spins you so fast, so hard that your brain rattles inside your skull. Your angel wings contract, shrivel, and vanish into two red-hot arrows of pain lodged in your shoulder blades.

Without that point of light in the far distance, you would give up the act of breathing, let go of your hold on life.

But I did it—I traveled beside Phoenix and Dean and held on. The light opened up at last into a gentle halo surrounding us, lowering us gently to earth.

"So now we know," Dean told Iceman, who stood waiting for us in the barn entrance. "There was a full-on feud between the Thornes and the Rohrs. Those guys were at war."

I ought to have been glad to have the evidence, but the main feeling was fear.

"How are you doing now?" I asked Phoenix.

He stood exhausted in the shadow of the barn, his supernatural energies drained and at an all-time low. His breathing was shallow, his beautiful, clear eyes dull. "I'm doing good," he lied.

Iceman came across, slung Phoenix's arm around his shoulder, and helped him into the barn, where he sat him on the steps. Dean and I followed. I crouched beside Phoenix and stroked his hand. "You need to rest," I whispered, trying to ease the ache that lingered beneath my shoulder blades.

"And think," Dean urged. His face had the steadfast, solemn, stony look. I guess it was the responsibility of becoming overlord—the weight of steering the Beautiful Dead's eternal future. "Try to remember—did this incident at the warehouse ever come up between you and your brothers? Is it something you were aware of?"

Phoenix let his head hang low. "I don't remember exactly."

There was a pause then Dean said, "I need the truth."

As always, Phoenix recognized that he couldn't deceive his overlord. "Maybe Brandon…one time, he might have mentioned it."

"Good. And did he ask you to watch out for Zak?"

"Again, it's not clear. But yeah, I guess."

This was so not like Phoenix that I asked Dean to hold back. "He's exhausted. He can't take any more questions."

Nodding abruptly, Dean eased me back for a consultation. "This sure looks like a motive," he said.

"Nathan is the kind of kid to keep hold of a grudge and let it fester."

"Until it drives him crazy," I agreed. "Pretty soon he would be out there looking for payback. And in his devious brain, harming Phoenix and making the whole Rohr family suffer forever would be the ideal way to do it."

"It worked," I said flatly, thinking of the twelve months of hell Nathan had put Sharon, Michael, Brandon, and Zak through.

"So that's it—we think we have the answer." Iceman was at the door, looking up at the mountains and watching the sun sink until only a rim of molten gold lay on the black horizon. "Nathan Thorne sees the scene at the gas station as a trigger for revenge. He jumps at the chance of striking back at Brandon, and since that's not enough, he pulls a knife and stabs his brother."

Out of the months of chaos and doubt came a simple, solid solution. It matched my gut feeling—Nathan Thorne was guilty. He killed Phoenix for revenge.

But Iceman, always in the background, always reliable, turned back toward us. "It doesn't feel like the end," he told the overlord. "I still think there's more."

12

Maybe it's because Dean had been a cop that he listened to Iceman. It was the investigator in him, the professional who checks and double-checks his facts.

"No jury would convict Nathan on the evidence we have," he agreed. We'd moved Phoenix from the barn to the house, put logs on the fire, and lit the oil lamps. I was watching his every move, following every breath he took.

"A strong motive and a history of violence between the Rohrs and the Thornes doesn't automatically mean a guilty verdict."

"But you heard the threat. Nathan said no one walks away! That means he was planning to kill them." I was against Iceman. I needed what we'd seen to be enough.

"But he didn't say Phoenix's name," Dean reminded me. "Only Brandon and Zak. We didn't get exactly what we needed."

"So we go back again," I urged. "Tonight, right now!"

Dean took a while before he made his next move, pacing the room, making the floorboards creak. He stopped on the bloodstained spot where Hunter had fallen long ago. "Another trip—will you make it?" he asked Phoenix.

Phoenix half closed his eyes and took a sharp breath, as if he was in pain. His face was drawn. "I don't know. Maybe."

I sat beside him, focused all my energy on him.

"Yes, you will," I told him softly. "So long as you keep on believing."

My words touched a nerve. He opened his eyes and smiled sadly. "So now *you* talk to *me* about belief!"

"I know. But it's true—belief is what it takes to get us through. You can make another trip. I know we can find the truth."

Phoenix closed his eyes again, and I wasn't sure that he'd taken in what I said. But when he opened them, he looked up at Dean. "I'm ready," he said.

❧

This is it—my last journey through time, the extraordinary trip that begins with beating wings as we stand in the yard under a starlit sky. The stars seem to drift then fall toward the ground, the ground dissolves, and I feel a tingling sensation at my shoulder blades. The starry mist, the beating wings surround me as I stand with Dean and Phoenix. I join the world of the Beautiful Dead and spread my magical white wings.

I am surrounded by starlight. I beat my angel wings in a

universe of lost souls—all those wings, souls without a voice, and me hand in hand with my beloved Phoenix.

The glow of the stars fades. We fly with the lost souls and enter a dark, spinning space, the eye of an unnatural hurricane, more powerful, more deathly than any earthly storm. I see a million death-heads. Skulls crowd in on me, grinning, sightless, flashing by. So many skulls in the vastness of the dark universe and every one attached to a soul in torment. They long for me to let go of Phoenix's hand, for him to be sucked into the dark vortex, to spin away into infinity.

"Hold on," Phoenix whispers. "Look ahead at the light." I see the pinprick of light. Dean leads the way, his wings spread wide. We follow, battered and torn.

It's a light like no other, out of thick blackness, growing stronger, pulling us on. The light opens up, defeats the darkness, and our wings thrust us spinning toward it. It surrounds us with an incandescent glow.

We're back in time twelve months to the Friday night when Phoenix died, standing in front of the gas station. At the roadside a red and green neon sign on top of a tall pole advertises gas for sale. In the small glass office Kyra sits behind her cashier's desk handing out receipts. A steady stream of customers fills their tanks without seeing us.

Dean leads Phoenix and angel-me between a line of cars to the awning over the entrance to the office where we have a clear view of the vehicles approaching the gas station in both directions. We stand beside a rack of newspapers and wait.

Three more cars swing into the forecourt and join the lines for gas. Jacob Miller arrives on a bicycle, dumps his bike by the door, and goes inside to buy candy and a Coke. Then a guy shows up on a Harley Softail, cruising around the edge of the lot, followed by a second rider on a Dyna. They get off their bikes. The second guy waits in line for gas while the other looks up and down the street. Beside me, Beautiful Dead Phoenix grows more alert.

Soon more Harleys arrive. I count three, four, five. The riders join the Softail guy, and they begin to laugh and joke.

Someone picks up a magazine and goes into the office to pay. With wings outspread, Phoenix stands between me and Dean, silently watching the minutes leading up to his own death.

A car crests the hill. Its headlights swoop toward us, past the white church and the psychiatric hospital into the gas station. Under the red light we recognize Nathan Thorne in his black Chevy. He joins the line nearest us, music blasting from his sound system.

Seconds later, Phoenix pulls up behind the first Dyna rider.

Beautiful Dead Phoenix sees his old living self sitting at the wheel of his truck with Zak beside him.

For a second I tell myself: Act now. Go to Phoenix, stop him from getting out of his truck. Change everything!

I believe in that moment that anything is possible, that I can cheat destiny after all. This is my chance to save Phoenix.

I feel my heart jolt. I know I have to grab the opportunity with both hands.

I can change this! *I silently tell my Beautiful Dead boyfriend.* There'll be no fight, no stabbing. You and I can go on living together…*In that moment, I believe this with all my heart. So I step out with my angel wings from under the awning, raise my hand, and put it on living Phoenix's arm.*

His skin is warm. I say, "Leave now, before it's too late."

Living Phoenix walks right through me without seeing me. He goes up to the guy ahead of him in the line and says, "I need gas in a hurry. Is it OK for me to go ahead?"

The guy tells him no, wait in line like everyone else.

I still want to believe I have the power to change history. My heart hammers, my mouth is dry.

"Turn around, walk away. If you don't want to die you have to leave," angel-me pleads.

Phoenix jumps back in his truck, reverses, then pulls up behind Nathan Thorne.

"Get out of here!" I cry, leaning against Phoenix's door to stop him from getting out.

Dean steps out from under the awning, pulls me back. He shakes his head. "Phoenix can't see you," he tells me. "He can't hear you. You don't exist."

I close my eyes, swallow hard, feel the frantic energy drain away as Dean pulls me back. It was a moment when I could have healed all wounds, mopped up all the tears, but it's gone.

Customers line up inside, more bikes arrive. Oscar Thorne's Mercedes sweeps into the station followed by Vince Hall and Robert Black. From the opposite direction, Brandon arrives on his Dyna. Ignoring Thorne and the others, he goes straight into the store to talk with Kyra.

"Man, I'm in a hurry," Phoenix tells Nathan as music blares. Jacob has bought his candy. He's left his bicycle in a bad place. A biker customer goes inside to pay, comes out, trips over the bike. He picks it up and throws it against the newspaper stand. There is a clash of metal. Jacob comes out yelling and cursing. The customer puts his hand in his face and pushes him over.

"Yeah, and I'm in line ahead of you," Nathan sneers at Phoenix as the fight begins. "I'm taking my time, see?" And he leans into his car, into the clash of drums and whine of guitars, making a big deal of looking for something. A small plastic envelope falls from the glove compartment onto the ground by Phoenix's feet. Phoenix stoops and picks it up.

Now Zak gets out of the truck to snatch the envelope. He says something to Phoenix that we don't hear above the music and the noise of the fight developing by the newsstand.

Jacob has half a dozen buddies on mountain bikes who appear out of nowhere, from side streets and from the main drag. They include Taylor Stafford, who skids to a halt and starts to kick someone's Dyna, knocking it over and stamping on the mirrors and wheels. Another kid picks up a garbage can and swings it at another's head. The kid is grabbed from behind.

By now there is a smell of spilled gas and ordinary customers are backing out of the station and driving away. Inside the store, Kyra waves Brandon aside and picks up the phone.

Nathan stops searching in his car and stands up straight.

"Give me back that packet," he demands. "Hey, Oscar— Zak took the envelope!"

Phoenix steps across Nathan's path. The fight outside the office is out of control, and now he loses it with Nathan. "Forget the envelope—move your car!" he demands, fists clenched.

Nathan tilts his head back and grins. "Make me," he says.

Zak moves in and quickly hands the packet to Nathan, who doesn't thank him but laughs in his face. Brandon strides out of the store toward them, through the brawling kids, past Oscar, Hall, and Black. He punches Nathan then grabs hold of Zak's collar and marches him onto the street, sends him sprinting off toward town. When he comes back, Phoenix has been surrounded by the younger kids, who are being forced back toward the road. Jacob and Taylor smash windshields and slash tires as they retreat.

A woman passenger stranded inside a white car begins to scream. Brandon has stopped to calm her, leaning an arm against the roof of her car, when Nathan opens his trunk and pulls out an iron bar. Blood runs from his nose as he charges at Brandon, wielding the bar over his head.

Glass shatters, tires hiss, the woman continues screaming.

Invisible, helpless, we watch as Oscar, Hall, and Black draw knives from their belts.

Nathan uses the metal bar to strike Brandon on the back of his head. Brandon staggers away from the white car into the path of Oscar Thorne. Phoenix breaks free of Jacob, Stafford, and the brawling kids and runs to catch Brandon as he falls.

Nathan comes at them again with the metal bar, this time with Oscar at his side. A passing kid rides his bike at Oscar's legs, sends him off balance, crashing into a gas pump and losing hold of his knife. Phoenix picks up the blade from the oil-stained ground. Nathan's bar misses Brandon and strikes the hood of the white car. Brandon stumbles clear.

There is a pause, a moment of thinking that it's all over, but it's only so that everyone can regroup.

Still with Oscar's knife in his hand, Phoenix faces Nathan, who is now flanked by Hall and Black. Nathan's nose is still bleeding, his face streaked scarlet.

The demented bike kids are wrecking cars and Harleys.

Taylor sets fire to a narrow trail of leaking gas, raising a tongue of flame across the station's lot that flares, lights the whole scene, then fizzles out in a dark stain.

Now Black throws a spare knife to Oscar, who catches it.

That makes four armed guys versus Phoenix. Seeing this, Brandon bends sideways, slips a hand down his boot, and pulls out a short, pointed knife. Then he goes to stand by his brother.

Angel-me tears my attention from the unfolding scene and glances at Beautiful Dead Phoenix. The pain in his eyes is terrible—the helplessness, the not wanting to know what comes next.

Blades flash red in the neon light. Black and Hall jab at Phoenix and Brandon, who is still unsteady from Nathan's first blow. Drums clash, guitars whine from Nathan's Chevy.

Oscar lunges at Brandon with his knife. Brandon sways and sidesteps into Phoenix, who falls against a gas pump then spins quickly to face Nathan.

Blades glint again, bodies stagger and blunder. As Brandon advances shakily on Oscar, Hall thrusts Phoenix across his path.

Brandon raises his knife. His blade flashes down as Phoenix stumbles in front of him. He pushes the point between Phoenix's shoulder blades. Phoenix falls to the ground.

Phoenix lies bleeding, looking up at Brandon.

Angel-me cries out one sharp syllable. "No!"

Beautiful Dead Phoenix stands beside me, looks at his dying self then at Brandon, and he spreads his arms wide.

In an agony of realization, Brandon falls to his knees.

In the confusion, only he knows what he's done. Oscar pulls Nathan back. Black and Hall grab Oscar's knife from Brandon and run with it. All across the gas station lot, cars and Harleys start up, race away. The kids on bikes vanish down the side streets.

Brother, I forgive you! *Beautiful Dead Phoenix looks on and spreads his arms. The feathers in his wings flutter. He looks like a crucified angel.*

Out on the blacktop, Brandon holds Phoenix in his arms.

"Tell Darina I'm sorry," Phoenix whispers before the whine of sirens splits the black silence.

He lies bleeding to death, gazing up at the brother who has killed him.

❧

There was the journey back—the black vortex, the million tortured souls—but nothing so terrible as the knowledge we had gained.

Dean said nothing. He led the way into the darkness, beating his wings to rise above the awning up into the cloud-heavy sky. Phoenix and I followed, looking down at two small figures, one hunched, one sprawled on the ground, waiting for the paramedics in a pool of harsh neon light.

Clouds surrounded us, the figures below were hidden by mist that twisted and turned, wound itself around us and carried us into the dark tunnel where there were no stars, no skies or earth, only a spinning force that dragged us out of the past toward an unbearable present and the last good-bye.

I held Phoenix's hand, followed the overlord, closed my eyes, and prayed for it to end differently.

Let this not be true.

The forces of time tore at us. The death-heads reappeared.

Go back. Tell it a new way. Take the knife out of Brandon's hand. Put it in Nathan's or Oscar's—anybody's.

Spare us.

Skulls grinned and crowded in. We were hurting in body and soul.

Dean led, and Phoenix and I followed, turning, falling, tumbling toward the here-and-now blinding light, torn apart.

13

Iceman waited at the barn door, under the branching moose horns, beside the rusting truck. He reached out and offered me his hand.

"I'm OK," I gasped, looking around for Phoenix, who had slumped against the barn wall, head back and staring at the starlit sky.

Dean stood a few paces from him, watchful and still silent.

I ran to Phoenix and led him into the barn, willed him to bring his attention back to me as I took his hands in mine. "Talk to me!" I whispered.

"This is how it ends," he murmured out of the musty darkness of dust and spiderwebs, a century of planting, harvest, and toil. "Not how we wanted, but how it was."

"I am so sorry!" I breathed. "I see now why you were afraid. And if I could alter it…if we could wipe it from our minds."

But his brother's name was branded there forever.

I put my trembling hands to Phoenix's ice-cold cheeks.

There was one more thing I needed to be sure of. "Did you know this from the beginning?" I asked.

There was no light in his dark eyes, no spark of comfort.

"No," he insisted. "After I left the house with Zak, there were a thousand fragments—faces, sounds, voices calling—but no clear knowledge."

"Did you suspect?"

He sighed. "A fight like that, a feud—I knew that anything was possible."

"Did Dean know?"

"He was a cop so he saw the files, he understood the background."

The overlord came into the barn with Iceman, watchful and still keeping his distance.

"Was Brandon's name on the list?" I asked Dean.

"Everyone who was there that night was a possible suspect, Brandon included." His answer fell heavily into the silence.

"And so what do I do now?" I demanded, turning in anger on Dean for the way things had worked out, hating the whole world for leaving me with the one answer I didn't expect. "Do I name Brandon? Do I say, 'Here's the guilty one'?"

The overlord stepped around us in a wide circle, his footsteps muffled, walking in deep shadow. "It's a tough call," he said quietly.

"Do I?" I asked Phoenix as gently as I could.

He sighed and shook his head. "We could have stepped

back from the brink," he reminded me. "We could have let it go."

I saw again the death-heads that had spun toward us in the time tunnel, desperate souls in a limbo of doubt, and I knew that stepping back from an answer would have meant that Phoenix would have joined them forever.

"No." I held on to the belief that I'd always had. "We needed to know."

"Darina's right," Iceman agreed. "Sometimes the truth hurts, but without it we can't move on."

We stood for a while in silence, except for the creak of hinges as the door swung open and closed. We were all waiting, holding our breaths. Phoenix was rapidly fading from me.

❧

"So what do I do?" I cried again.

Dean took me on one last journey, promising me that Phoenix would still be at Foxton when I got back.

"Wait for me," I begged in the midnight barn.

Phoenix's spirit was ebbing, was withdrawing from the far side like the tide pulling back from the shore. When he embraced me, I couldn't be sure how much longer his arms would have the strength to hold me.

"Be here," I pleaded.

Then Dean surrounded me in gentle light and carried

me away from Foxton, across the dark mountains to Deer Creek where he set me down under the stars. "Talk to Brandon," he told me. "Make your decision."

The overlord left me at the water's edge.

I waited where I had waited for Phoenix a year ago, by the big boulder in the middle of the creek. Stars shone over my head and in the stream at my feet.

In the dead of night Brandon rode out to meet me.

"I got your text," he said, laying his bike in the tall grass, standing uncertainly beside it, his jacket zippered to the chin, hands in pockets. "What's so urgent that it couldn't wait until tomorrow?"

"This couldn't," I murmured. I wanted to look into the face of the man who had killed his brother.

Brandon narrowed his gaze and walked down the steep bank toward me. "So?"

I stared at him, at the face of a guy whose suspicious eyes permanently said, *Don't come near me. Don't try to understand or fix me.*

The creek ran at our feet. We stared down at the shimmering reflection of the stars. "There's something I have to tell you," I murmured.

He looked away. The barrier stayed up.

"I know what happened a year ago."

Still no reaction. The water flowed on.

Say it quiet and clear in the electric midnight air. "You killed Phoenix."

If Brandon had made excuses, said it was a mistake, if he'd asked me how I knew or had tried to blame the Thornes or the confusion of that night, I might have had a clear idea of what to do next.

"It was you," I said again. And I saw Phoenix stumble across Brandon's path, I saw the blade go in. I saw it again and again.

Brandon stared at the black boulder and at the water rushing over rocks, splashing, churning, whirling on.

Talk to Brandon, Dean had said. *Make your decision.*

"You don't deny it?" I asked. Guilt didn't look the way I expected, shored up by excuses and anger.

Brandon shook his head. His voice seemed to be lost and swept away in the current.

"Why didn't you tell me?"

He gave me a dull, weary look then shrugged.

"How does it feel? Talk to me."

Walking away, crunching over the pebbles, walking back. "It feels like hell," he said.

Make your decision.

Brandon waited a long time to speak again. "Hell. I never leave it behind. I stay home, I hang out in town—it's with me every second. I ride into the mountains, and it's there.

267

I sleep and dream it. I want it to work out different. I wake up, and it's the same."

Make your decision.

I looked at Brandon and saw that he, not Phoenix, had joined those death-heads, spinning through a dark universe in eternal torment. I understood this and felt the first pang of pity.

"What about Sharon?" I asked. I compared her with Bob Jonson who had lost Jonas, with the Taylors grieving over Arizona, and with Jon and Heather Madison accepting that Summer was gone forever. "Doesn't your mom deserve to know?"

"How would it help?" Brandon muttered. He'd considered it a million times, never reached an answer.

I thought again about Bob Jonson. "I hear you."

A death wish sat heavy on Bob's shoulders after Jonas died, and the truth didn't lift it. It ended astride a Dyna in a soaring arc over the cliff edge, a plunge into white water and oblivion.

And how did it help Sharon to have Brandon stand in front of a jury? To know that if it had worked out a split second differently Phoenix might have lived?

Then again. "This is to do with justice." I sighed. "The others—Jonas, Arizona, and Summer—they got it, whatever it cost."

"Show me a way out," Brandon pleaded. "I mean it, Darina. An exit out of this is all I'm asking."

"I don't know that you get to ask for anything," I said more harshly. "That's not how it works." Because of Brandon we had all lived through twelve months of agony.

And suddenly, unexpectedly and out of nowhere, I was back for a delirious moment, here by Deer Creek with Phoenix, under the stars. It was our place, our precious time. I whispered his name. "Phoenix!"

Brandon heard me. He stood so still for so long I thought he'd stopped breathing.

I called Phoenix's name, but it was Dean who came to me. "I can't do this alone. You have to help me decide."

Dean stood on the far bank surrounded by light. He was tall, unbending in the moonlight. "Explain your thinking, Darina. But hurry—we have very little time."

"I feel sorry for Brandon. I didn't expect to."

"His is not a common suffering," the overlord agreed.

We gazed at him standing a little way off, a lonely figure under the stars.

"What happens if the killer walks free?" I asked Dean. "Will Phoenix still get to move on?"

"I understand—you need justice for Phoenix to secure his journey's end, but now you have to be prepared for things you didn't expect, to open your eyes to the fact that justice takes more than one form."

"I long for Phoenix to be free," I whispered. "It's all I ever wanted. I'm scared that if I don't name Brandon, Phoenix will be trapped in limbo."

"Does the world have to know the truth?" Dean asked. "Darina, I'm not sure. I don't have the answer." And he looked kindly at me, surrounded by his halo of light.

I walked up to Brandon with a big weight still on my shoulders, and I looked straight into his eyes.

He gazed back at me across a barrier of total, unending misery.

"You took a life, and you saved one," I said softly, knowing clearly and precisely now why Brandon had shown no fear as he ran into the flames.

"Without you, Zak would have died."

A brother's life taken. A brother's life saved.

Brandon heard me, walked a little way along the bank, turned, and when he came back, I saw that he was crying.

The weight lifted from my shoulders. *A life taken, a life saved.*

❦

I've kept the secret of the Beautiful Dead for twelve whole months, so carrying to my grave the knowledge of what Brandon did shouldn't be too much of a stretch.

"Tomorrow morning at dawn, ride out to Foxton to find me," I told him. "I'll need you then."

He wiped his tears then walked up the bank and rode off on his Harley. I waited until the sound of the engine died.

"Come with me," Dean said, inviting me into his silver glow.

We found Phoenix still in the barn, sitting on the hayloft steps with Iceman by his side.

"He has only a few minutes," Iceman warned, touching Phoenix lightly on the shoulder as he and Dean left us alone together.

And as I sat beside Phoenix, I knew we'd reached the moment I dreaded. Every minute, every hour, every day of the last year had been leading to this. Now it was here.

"I can't find the words," I whispered, a tight band of sorrow around my chest.

Phoenix put his finger to my lips. "What's left to say? Except, we lived our whole lives for each other."

"And you'll be free?"

"Like Jonas and the others."

"Will you see them again?"

"No one knows. All I'm sure of is that I leave the far side and go forward."

Out of the darkness into light, free from doubt.

I took his trembling hand in mine, felt the dampness of

my own tears on his cold fingertips. "Will I join you—in the end?"

Phoenix smiled, and the crooked curve of his lips caught at my heart. "Let's risk a yes on that," he murmured.

"And I know that we'll never be apart. Remember—as long as you live, when you need me I'll be there."

"Any time, any place?" I moved my lips, but no sound came out.

"In a heartbeat," he promised.

He leaned forward, and his lips touched mine—not a kiss exactly, only a brief, brushing contact before those searching, all-knowing eyes looked into mine one last time.

Then Dean and Iceman returned. They stood in the doorway, waiting for Phoenix to rise slowly from the step.

I held his hand, and I was the one who led the way out of the barn into the starlight before his time finally ran out, to the sound of the creek running through the valley and the sight of the crescent moon in a jeweled sky.

Phoenix walked slowly past the silver-gray ranch house, glancing at the shadowy porch and the securely bolted door. He smiled at me again.

In Hunter and Marie's time, at a different place in history, this is where we would live.

"I know."

Dean and Iceman hung back until the very last moment.

They let us reach the water's edge together.

"You are everything to me," I told Phoenix.

He kissed me on the lips, soft and cold. He spread his white wings and his hand slipped from mine.

And he walked away with his two companions, never turning back as they made their way out of the valley toward the ridge and the aspens, silver in the moonlight.

Three winged creatures walked into the shadows. The barn door swung closed. The Beautiful Dead departed.

Epilogue

Brandon came for me at dawn, and I drifted through days. Sharon Rohr visited our house before we left. She said that Zak's burns had healed and he would soon be back in school.

"Thank you," she told me, and our own deep wounds continued to heal.

Zoey heard through her dad that Michael Rohr was definitely sticking around for a while.

I didn't care. I was drifting, sinking, letting go of the world.

"Brandon sold his Harley," Hannah told me. "He bought a plane ticket to Europe."

I nodded. Maybe it would help him, but really, no— he and I both knew that. I didn't try to see him before he left.

Danny Kors found Oscar and Nathan Thorne holed up in the fisherman's shack at Forest Lake. His "clean up Ellerton" campaign was making real progress. People started to relax.

Henry Jardine drove out to Foxton and nailed planks

of wood across the barn door to keep out intruders. Kids camped out at Government Bridge undisturbed.

After Brandon brought me home from Foxton that Friday morning, I didn't step outdoors until the day we moved.

Our new porch overlooked the lake. The water was smooth and sky blue.

Still I was sinking beneath its surface, and nothing would stop me.

I feel like I'm drowning. I go down in the clear, cold water without a struggle—this time no one holds me under, I am letting myself sink. Above me bubbles rise to the surface, and beyond that is a bright, quivering light that must be the sun.

It's far away. My hair spreads like weeds, my legs and arms are weightless, water all around. My eyes are wide open, staring at the light. A current catches me and turns me facedown, staring into darkness. It plunges me deeper, twists me again until I glimpse the dappled, liquid light farther and farther above me.

And suddenly, without knowing why, I strike out. I forge upward, my arms cleaving the icy water, its whisper in my ears. I kick and fight back.

I choose life.

"I want you to take this." Michael Rohr showed up at our new house with the picture he'd once shown me of Brandon and Phoenix. "It belongs with you."

I took it and put it in my bedside drawer.

Who needs a picture on display when you have memories like mine to bear you up and carry you through life?

Any time, any place? I ask, gazing out across the glittering lake.

A breeze disturbs its silver surface. *In a heartbeat,* Phoenix promises.

About the Author

Eden Maguire lives part of the time in the United States where she enjoys the big skies and ice-capped mountains of Colorado. Eden Maguire's lifelong admiration for Emily Brontë's timeless classic, *Wuthering Heights*, ties in with her fascination for the dark side of life and informs her portrayal of the restless, romantic souls in *Beautiful Dead*. Aside from her interest in the supernatural and the solitary pursuit of writing fiction, Eden's life is lived as much as possible in the outdoors, thanks to ranch-owning friends in Colorado. She says, "Put me on a horse and point me toward a mountain—that's where I find my own personal paradise."